HIDING PLACES

SKYE WARREN

CHAPTER ONE

Jane Mendoza

T HE SMELLS OF roasted coffee and warm sugar waft over me as I step inside.

A little bell rings above the door. Dark wood furniture mixes in haphazardly with lumpy cushion chairs. Original paintings from a local artist hang on the walls with handwritten business cards beside them, with an email address and price. It's quiet in the mid-afternoon.

A woman sits with her young child, the remnants of a muffin split between them on the table. Each of them has a book. There's a pang of sadness inside me.

That could have been me and Paige.

A man works on his laptop. There's a thick backpack in the seat opposite him that looks like it must weigh 100 pounds. He brings forth a different kind of envy.

I want that sense of purpose.

The barista looks up from her phone with a friendly smile. She has the kind of wispy red hair and pale, freckled skin that I've always admired. A small, scalloped nose ring looks effortlessly cool. "Good morning. What can I get ya?"

I study the large chalkboard menu hanging above us as if this is a more important choice than a drink. "A caramel macchiato," I say. "Please."

"Hot or iced?"

I press my lips together. I'm not used to ordering five-dollar lattes. I'm not used to wearing two-hundred-dollar faux fur boots. I'm not used to having a brand-new wardrobe full of perfectly fitting new clothes in every modern style.

There's a cute retro headband in my hair. When I saw the price tag, I nearly had a heart attack. Beau Rochester doesn't ask for permission. These clothes simply appear in my closet. No receipt, no bags, no way to send them back.

The only thing I can do is wear them.

"Iced," I finally say.

She takes my money and then gestures toward a counter where I can wait. Her hands work efficiently at the silver levers on a complicated machine. Big rumbly sounds erupt along with a frothy drink. Someone else comes in and before they've even made it to the counter, the barista grins at them. "The usual?" she asks.

"God, yes," the woman says, juggling a large tote and a toddler. "How's Benny?"

"Same old," the barista says.

"Well, tell him if he ever wants a job he is always welcome at the bakery. For that matter, you should come work for me too, Simone."

Simone, that's her name.

This isn't the kind of establishment where she has a name tag on her green apron. This is the kind of place where everyone already knows her name, where she knows everyone's order without them having to read a chalkboard menu.

In some ways, I fit into this new world. I have money now, and clothes that fit, but I still don't belong. When my drink is ready, I wave my thanks and find a small table in the corner.

My tote bag contains college applications. Not one, not two.

There are over fifty in this massive stack.

I can't decide where I want to go so I figured I'd let the colleges decide for me. Fifty applications, loads of essays. It's a lot. Too much, even. But it's a distraction that I need. A project to keep my heart from breaking now that I don't get to see Paige every single minute.

The first one is a small private college in up-state Maine.

Name one person who influenced you.

My mind immediately flies to Beau, the man who rescued me, the man I rescued in return.

I also think of Noah, my friend from the foster home. He helped me more than I can repay.

In the end, it's Paige that I write about. An anonymous little girl who started off as a nanny job but ended up stealing my heart. I lose myself in the paperwork and drain my drink down to the ice cubes. I don't realize how much time has passed.

The bell over the door tinkles. A shadow blocks the light.

"What can I get ya?" the barista asks, the same way she asked me. This person is also a stranger. Except when I look up, he's familiar.

Beau Rochester orders a large coffee, black.

He sits down across from me before it's ready. "Any good ones?" he asks.

"Yes," I say, but it's not exactly an agreement.

He doesn't think I should apply to 50 schools. He wants me to apply to my dream school. That's it. I always thought that if I went to college anywhere, it would be in Texas. The University of

Texas at Austin has an amazing social work division. Plus, it made the most sense location wise. The in-state tuition would have been the most affordable. So I built my visions of college around wearing burnt orange.

Dreams change. Beau taught me that. Paige taught me that too.

I can't imagine being so far away from her. More than that, I can't imagine taking Beau so far away from her. He doesn't want me to compromise, but it isn't a compromise to stay in Maine.

The barista emerges from the counter and hands Beau his coffee. He accepts it with a murmured, "Thanks."

The barista, Simone, continues to stand there. "You're Rhys Rochester's brother?" It's not exactly a friendly question, but there's no avarice in her voice.

It strikes me that I'm not the only outsider here.

Beau was born on these shores, but he didn't stick around. He made his fortune on the West Coast. It was his brother who stayed here, his brother who would have been known by the barista, his brother who died an ignoble death after working with a dirty cop.

We are more than outsiders in this small

Maine town. We're infamous.

Headlines splashed when a former detective was charged with Rhys Rochester's murder.

For his part, Beau has been stoic.

He doesn't want to talk about the fact that his brother abused his wife or the fact that he helped steal drugs and property as a dirty cop. He doesn't want to talk about it, but it eats at him.

"That's me," Beau says, his expression grim.

I tense, waiting for the barista to say something sharp or condemning. Instead, she gives a friendly smile. "Tell Paige I said hi. And that I have a cookie with sprinkles waiting for her whenever she drops by again."

Beau nods.

The barista disappears, and then I'm left with a man I love and a paper stack of possibility.

He picks up one of the papers and reads aloud. "*Reflect on a time when you faced an unexpected challenge. How did you deal with it and what did you learn from the experience?*" He reads my answer quietly and then sets the paper down. "Hell."

My cheeks flush, "I didn't think you were going to read that."

"You couldn't have written about the time you showed up for your job rain-logged and exhausted, and I pushed a kitten at you? 'Keep it alive,' I said. 'Consider this your interview.'"

I worry my nail into the edge of the desk where the glue has started to separate. "It was intense," I say, "but not really unexpected. I was getting paid a lot for this nanny job. It was always going to be hard."

"Jane."

I sigh and close my eyes. The money is incredible. He didn't just pay me my one-year salary. He insists on showering me with money, with gifts.

He even wanted to hire this super expensive college coach because apparently that's a thing rich people can do. The person would manage my applications, including all the deadlines and the recommendations. They would also do deep edits of all of my essays.

I refused. The money is hard enough to take without additional help.

"Money doesn't mean anything," Beau says.

"That's what people with money say."

The money was an unexpected challenge.

That's what I wrote in this short essay question. Yes, it's also a boon, a gift, a freaking miracle. It means I can go to college anywhere that I want. It means I'll be able to focus on my studies instead of having to work three jobs to pay the rent.

It's an incredible blessing in my life, but it also forces me to face my deepest fears that I can't do this on my own. I want to be with Beau because I love him and because he loves me, not because I need him to achieve my goals.

I wrinkle my nose at him. "I thought you had a meeting this morning."

"It was cut short," he says, a gleam in those storm gray eyes, "when I got a call from the builder. It's ready."

Excitement races down my spine, along with a touch of uncertainty. The house means setting down roots. *Even if you go to college somewhere else*, Beau said, *we'll always have the house near Paige.* I want that, but I'm also quietly terrified.

Back when I worked for Beau at Coach House, taking care of Paige, it was kind of like playing house. We were a pretend family, but now, even though we've lost Paige, we're no longer playing house. This is real.

And Beau? He's my family.

CHAPTER TWO

Beau Rochester

"CAN I OPEN my eyes?" Jane asks. She's got one hand blocking her vision and a big grin on her face. "You know, I've seen the plans for the house. I've been here lots of times."

"It's different." I want to remember her in this moment. Happy. Excited. Our new house has been under construction for months. Building a house seems like it should be straightforward. Approve the plans. Hire contractors. Break ground. Things come up, though. Problems to be solved. Decisions you didn't think you'd have to make. Delays. Now we're finally standing in front of the completed home, next to my car in the driveway. "Yes. Go ahead."

Jane takes her hand away and looks up at the house. A little gasp comes from her lips. "It's perfect," she says. "Look, Beau. It's our house."

I put an arm around her waist and pull her into my side. "Yes, it is."

I'm trying not to let on that this house is a goddamn miracle. My life with Jane is a miracle. She had no reason to stand by me after the way I treated her when we first met. I was a sullen asshole who was so hurt he couldn't see straight. I'm still an asshole. No one would argue that she turned me into a teddy bear. But it's impossible to be sullen when she's smiling like that.

"It's just how we wanted."

Actually, it's not just how we wanted.

There was a shortage of the paint color for the exterior, so it's a different shade of white. Half the shutters on the windows came in the wrong pattern so we switched them out midway through construction. Who the hell cares? If it's right in Jane's eyes, it's right.

Looks pretty good to me, too. We share a property line with the boundary of Coach House's grounds. The rebuilt Coach House is in sight of ours. Most importantly, it's within running distance for Paige. She can leave the door of Coach House and come over without going out of view for a second. Paige and Emily have a space that's all theirs. Refreshed and new, without any hauntings or bad memories. Coach House has the same massive, cliffside shape as it always did. It was registered as a historical property, so when it was rebuilt, it had to be to the old specifications. Updated electric, of course. Modern safety features. Traditional design.

Jane shades her eyes with her hand and looks over our house. In shape, it's more modern to Coach House. That kind of design made the most sense. Ours isn't as large, and it's much lighter, both in paint colors and actual light. Windows everywhere. Stunning views. Enough bedrooms to have Paige stay over. Paige and guests, even.

"Let me show you the inside." I'm nervous for her to see it. Not all of it will be a surprise to her, but some things will. I want her to love this place. If she doesn't, I'll tear the whole thing down and start again.

"Okay," she agrees.

Jane has seen the plans for the interior, but not the actual progress as we've worked. She follows me like an excited puppy. A wide, sunny foyer welcomes us into the house. Stairs lead up to the second floor.

"Straight back is the kitchen." I can see the countertops from here. "Living room's on our left."

"Show me the bedrooms," Jane says. "Then

we'll come back downstairs." We go up together, Jane taking the stairs two at a time. "It smells so nice in here," she says with a sigh.

"It smells new. It smells like paint."

She laughs. "I like it." I like it, too. At Coach House, I was always looking over my shoulder. My brother's presence seemed like it was part of the walls there. Part of the furniture. Here, everything is for us. Jane turns a corner into a bedroom. "Paige?" she asks.

"Yeah."

"Oh my God," she breathes. "She's going to love it."

We did her room in a Monopoly theme. One of the walls is painted to look like a giant Monopoly game board. She's got a full-size bed with Monopoly throw pillows and an oversized stuffed thimble piece. Jane runs her palm over the dresser, then goes out to see the other guest rooms. One blue, one green. And then, at the back of the house, the master.

Jane's eyes get huge. "This is way bigger than it looked on the plans."

Sunlight pours in from windows that overlook the ocean. On one end of the room is a sitting area. A couch with a blanket thrown over the back and two chairs. A bookshelf. A table. At the other end is our new bed. Jane touches the end of the comforter lightly with her fingertips.

"This is like a fancy hotel."

"It won't feel like a hotel once we're here for a few nights."

Jane gets on tiptoe to kiss me. "I just meant that it's beautiful," she murmurs against my mouth. "Anywhere you are feels like home."

She's astonished at the size of the bathroom and our walk-in closets. Delighted at the hand-carved wooden floors and thick carpets. At the small architectural details throughout. Her joy is the first thing to enter the rooms since they've been completed.

I can't think of anything better.

Jane pauses one more time at the door to the master bedroom, and I take her in my arms. "We could spend the rest of the day in bed."

She turns her body to kiss me back. "We haven't seen the rest of the downstairs yet."

I only agree because there is something I want to show her. Something that wasn't included in the plans. The space was there, but not the final details. I chose those myself.

Jane twines her fingers through mine and pulls me down the stairs with her. We turn toward the kitchen and go down the hall. She peeks into my office, but I put my hands on her shoulders and guide her past.

The kitchen is large and light soaked. It would draw most women, but Jane sees the room I'm most proud of the second we step inside.

"Beau," she gasps. "What is that?"

"A sunroom."

It's off the kitchen. Technically, off the living room, too.

It's a vaulted room, impossibly high on one side, sloping down into a series of wide, slanted windows that look up through the trees. It continues down with a wall of windows, broken only by French doors. It feels like we're standing on a calm version of the cliff—there's a clear view of the sea. The designer I hired from New York has added live plants in the corners. A few black-and-beige prints of a nautilus. A small white-globe light hanging from the ceiling will provide only enough light to read when it gets dark.

She'll still be able to see the stars.

"This is my favorite spot," she says, climbing into the king-sized futon, complete with matching throw pillows and a large oversized knit blanket. Already an end table contains a stack of books, and she runs her fingers down the spines.

I want her fingers on me. "Your favorite spot?

Not the bedroom?"

"My second-favorite spot, then," she says with an impish grin.

"There's something else."

"More than this?" Jane stands and walks to the kitchen. She opens her arms wide and twirls beneath the skylights. "I thought you were keeping things simple."

"It is simple."

I lead her back through the kitchen and stop at the first door on the right. Jane opens it and tiptoes in. "You wanted *two* offices?"

"It's for you." A real, honest-to-God office. Floor-to-ceiling shelves. A sturdy desk by a window that looks out on the side yard. An armchair for comfort. "You need a place other than the coffee shop or the sofa to do your work."

"I barely have any work yet." Her dark eyes are bright with happiness even as she tries to convince me that she doesn't need this. "Applications and essays."

"It's important work." I take her face in my hands and kiss her. Jane's sweet and warm. I could kiss her every second for the rest of my life and it wouldn't be enough. "It's how you'll take the next step. And once you've chosen that, you'll have this place to come back to. It's all yours."

"Let me see your office. Let me see where you'll be when I'm in here."

"It's on the other side of that wall."

"No door?" Jane's pout isn't serious, but if I could, I'd punch through the wall and make a door right now. "I guess it's better for focus."

"It's why we have separate rooms. If I could see you, I wouldn't be able to keep my hands off you."

I can't keep my hands off her now. We go over to my office. Jane gets quieter as we approach my desk. "This room is just like you. It's serious. A little… dangerous."

"Dangerous? The desk?"

"The man." She leans against the desk, her hands curling around the edge. Jane did this on purpose. We're down here because of the thrill. And because we've done things in my office before. Things that are too filthy for a sweetheart like Jane. "It makes me want you."

Everything makes me want her. She can't take a breath without me wanting her. She can't put on a shirt in the morning or wiggle her hips into sleep shorts at night without me wanting to fuck her. I should have more control over my urges at this point in life. Jane Mendoza has demolished that idea. I'm at the mercy of her.

"You didn't like the bedroom?"

"I love the bedroom." She watches me get closer. Tips her face up as I cage her against the desk. "I like your office, too."

"With the door wide open like this?" We're alone in the house, but she likes the suggestion of an illicit game. "Anyone could see you. Or hear you. There's nothing to block the sound."

"You're the only one I care about."

✧   ✧   ✧

Jane Mendoza

BEAU'S ARMS ARE like a cage. They hold me in place. There's a touch of fear, but that only drives the desire hotter.

"Do you remember?" he asks. "Do you remember when you came in my office?" There's dark knowledge in his eyes and I know exactly what he's talking about.

It feels like my cheeks are on fire. Without breaking eye contact, I shake my head no. "I don't remember." It's a lie and it's also a challenge. I want him to remind me.

The corner of his mouth lifts. He reaches back to hold my hair, his fist tightens until it tugs my scalp, until tears sting my eyes. He leans close and licks at my lips. Bites at them.

It's not a sweet kiss, it's aggressive.

And my body reacts, readying itself for him.

I'm already halfway to orgasm and he's barely even touched me. He definitely hasn't touched me between my legs. He won't, if this is anything like last time.

"Let me remind you," he says, the words low against my lips.

And then his hand directs me down, down, down until my knees touch the ground.

They're straddling his shoes, the same brown dress shoes that probably cost some ungodly amount of money, probably imported from Italy.

"Go ahead," he says, his eyes glittering with sexual menace. "Make yourself feel good."

I'm too embarrassed. It was one thing to do it in his dark office at Coach House. This one is full of light. No one's watching, but anyone could see me.

His expression says he knows. He knows, but there isn't going to be any mercy. He taps two fingers against my cheek in command. "Bear down, sweetheart. You know how to begin. You did it so well before. You did it so sweetly, humping your pretty cunt on my shoe, holding my leg, riding me for all you're worth. You remember now, don't you?"

I let out a jagged breath. "Yes," I say unsteadi-ly.

He waits with endless patience. I can see the bulge in his slacks. I can see his arousal, but it doesn't change anything. This is for me, which makes it somehow more humiliating that I should derive my pleasure in this way.

I rock my hips experimentally. The pressure feels wrong.

His fingers, his mouth, his cock. I've been spoiled by a man who knows how to please me.

But this? This is awkward. And ironically that's what makes it hotter.

I rock again and close my eyes.

"No," he says. "Watch me."

I look into his eyes, into their fathomless depth, as I press my sex to the top of his shoe, again and again, until climax overtakes me in a sudden, bright, almost painful burst.

CHAPTER THREE

Emily Rochester

I DON'T LIKE the courthouse.

I've never liked it, from the time I went to school here. The building's the same style as most of the city buildings, but something about the courthouse just feels foreboding and vaguely threatening. It's one of those places where your life can be made or ruined.

Neither of those things happened to me today, unless your life is ruined if you have to testify against your brother, which I did.

It's over now, and I want to leave. Paige is with Beau and Jane, and I want to get back to her. I want to get back to anywhere that's not this trial, and this courthouse. Anywhere I can be with my daughter and out from under the dark cloud of my brother's actions.

Getting out won't be easy.

I mean to exit the courthouse at full speed. It's not an option. Reporters crowd around the door. They stand in front of it and block me from opening it all the way, and when they let me out, they're like snapping dogs.

Not the kind of crowd you'd probably see in a big city, but enough of one that my stomach turns over. I don't want to have to push my way through them. Step close enough and they converge on you. They're not afraid to jostle.

I hold my purse tighter and try to keep my head down. It's pointless. I'm the woman who came back from the dead. I testified against my brother. Shutters click, again and again and again until I want to scream.

One voice cuts through the others. A voice I hate. This photographer is always pushy. Always in my face.

"How did it feel to go against your own family today, Emily?" he shouts. He's so loud. "What message do you think this sends to your daughter?"

"No comment." I want to say more. I want to tell him to shut the hell up about Paige and never mention her name again, but then that's the story.

"Where is your daughter today, Emily? Is it true your custodial rights have been reinstated?"

He does this on purpose. It's the man's one skill, and he's relentless at it. The rapid-fire questions are meant to be frustrating, and they are. I hate his questions. That's how he gets people to answer.

"Leave me alone." They're making it hard to get through, like they always do, but today it's hard to breathe. Maybe it's a bigger crowd than I thought. They press closer.

"Did you testify to cover up for Beau Rochester?"

The photographer steps fully into my path. It would be laughable if we were on the open sidewalk. That he has to resort to this to make a living. But we're not. I'm hemmed in on both sides. My heart thuds with panic, the same way it did when Rhys would hit me. All I could think about was keeping him calm and doing whatever he wanted and making it safe for Paige.

It's going to be like this forever, I think, helplessness squeezing at my heart and my lungs. It's just going to last and last until I can't take it anymore.

A shadow blocks the sun. Someone even closer. At first it startles me, but then I see who it is.

Not a reporter. Mateo.

He stands close, his arm making a barrier

around me. "Leave her alone. You've had enough. Back up. Back up *now*."

They listen to him. He's obviously used to dealing with photographers and paparazzi, but his voice has an edge of quiet fury. It almost seems like he's pissed off on my behalf, which can't be possible. Right now I don't care. I just want to get out of here, even if Mateo Garza has to be the one to help me.

And he does. He shepherds me through the crowd and to his car, which is waiting at the curb. It's parked illegally. He opens the door for me, throwing a death glare over his shoulder at the reporters. I get in.

We're flying through town by the time I catch my breath.

"Why didn't you have someone escort you out? You had to know they'd be out there." Mateo's tone isn't cruel, but it's not kind, either.

"I thought it would be fine." I mean to snap at him, but it comes out shaken instead. I don't want to make a scene in the courtroom, ever, so I've been holding myself in check for hours. Testifying was a nightmare. Joe sat right there and he heard every word. And then that asshole outside. I knew it wouldn't be fine. Nothing is going to be fine until all of this is finished. I hoped it would be fine. Sometimes it's all I can do.

"You know, you can plan ahead for this. You don't have to put yourself in that situation."

"Oh, yeah? I can just call down to the police station and ask them to help me?"

Mateo cuts a glance my way. "It doesn't have to be the police. You know how to do this."

"I shouldn't have to." It's true. I shouldn't have to hire private security because my brother's a criminal.

I shouldn't have to do any of this. One tear spills out onto my cheek. I wasn't going to cry. I was going to handle everything today like the competent, capable woman I am. Prove to the world, or at least the people in the courtroom, that I'm not a liar. That I'm not a woman gone crazy.

Another tear falls, and I turn my face to the window to hide it.

He sees anyway.

"Emily."

I don't answer. I'm holding my breath so I don't make any noise. Mateo's been driving to my house—he knows the way—but he puts on his turn signal and turns. Toward the beach. It's three minutes at most and more tears fall, one by one, hot on my skin.

He stops the car. I can't look at him. I don't want to see his pity or his judgment. I chose to marry Rhys. I didn't choose the rest. If it were up to me, none of this would have happened. Today wouldn't have been so hellish. He steps out of the car and closes the driver's side door behind him. I keep my eyes on the dashboard.

My door opens a second later.

He's blurred by my tears, looking down at me. If I open my mouth, if I say one word to Mateo Garza, I'll break. Everything will come out. I can't do it. I can't tell him. I can't name these feelings. I can't label the swirling vortex of fear inside or I'll crumble.

Mateo waits. It's better here, with the waves on the shore and the salt smell in the air, but I can't put the tears away. I can't force them back.

A sob escapes. I tremble around it. There are more coming.

Mateo leans down, unbuckles my belt, and pulls me out of the car. I'm not sure he means to hug me. I'm not sure he wants to. But he's the only person there when I break down. There's nobody else. I expect him to mock me. Or at least remain distant. Instead he pulls me close. I'm in his arms when I shatter into a thousand pieces.

I'm held together in impassible strength. His embrace both tears down my walls and gives me shelter.

CHAPTER FOUR

Jane Mendoza

"JAIL," SAYS PAIGE, a little smile on her face. Jail for me, of course. She hasn't gone to jail once this entire game of Monopoly. Meanwhile I've been behind bars four times. It's unheard of.

"Jail again," I agree. I'd rather be in Monopoly jail across from Paige than anywhere else.

This is the kind of thing that wouldn't come so easily if I move away for college. The option is still there, of course. I haven't decided anything yet. Haven't even heard back from most places. But the decision looms in my mind. Back in Houston, paying for college would be the tough part. The decision itself was easy. I'd have gone to the University of Texas without a second thought.

Now what? We have a brand-new house in Eben Cape, close enough to the new Coach

House that Paige can run over whenever she wants. Or when Emily needs us to watch her, like today.

A car pulls up outside, tires crunching on gravel.

Paige's eyes light up. "It's Mom."

She abandons the game and runs for the door. We've been sitting on the floor at the coffee table for long enough that my knees protest when I rise. Hazards of Monopoly, I guess.

Along with endless trips to jail.

Outside, Paige has her arms wrapped around Emily's waist, hugging her like she's been gone for years instead of a few hours. My heart warms. They belong together.

Paige's bright smile captures my attention at first.

It takes me a moment to understand that something's wrong.

Emily's been crying. Her eyes are red. Something must have happened. Joe's trial has been tough for her the entire time. Then today she had to get sworn in, facing him across a courtroom. How bad could it have gone? Did he say something rude? Surely the judge wouldn't allow that. Did the defense attorney badger the witness?

I step into the summer breeze. "Everything

okay?"

She gives me a grim smile. "I'm still standing. That has to count for something."

"It counts for a lot," I say, my voice softening so Paige doesn't hear. She's drawing designs into the pebbles on the drive. She's resilient, but she doesn't need to hear the details of how her uncle murdered her father. Or the resulting court trial. She gets that resiliency from her mother, who's overcome an abusive relationship and a state of hiding before being free. "Do you want me to keep her for a little longer? We can always play another round."

"No," she says, a little too loud. It's still hard for her to leave Paige. I can't even imagine what it was like for her to be away from her child for so long. Unbearable. "No, thank you. I really appreciate you watching her, but I'm fine now."

Which of course confirms that she was *not* fine earlier today. "What happened?"

Emily's blue eyes are fixed on Paige. "The usual, I expect."

For a murder trial, she means. And she's pretending to be fine. I know she's lying. She's clearly fragile, and I want to wrap her in a hug—but we aren't close enough for that. "Let me know if I can do anything."

"I will," Emily says, though that's also a lie. I suppose living that long in the shadow of violent men has made her protective of the truth. She looks past me, out toward where the ocean is a glittering blue. Summer in Eben Cape is basically the real-life version of a tourism brochure for Maine. It's all green grass and ocean waves and the breeze rustling in the trees. Summer is what makes the winters here worth it. I almost wish this trial wasn't happening at the most beautiful time of year. "I was holding it together. At least I thought I was. Until the reporter."

"A reporter?" I hadn't even thought about that. We live in Eben Cape, not a busy city. We have a local paper. And a radio station that's in the next town over.

"I can't even remember what outlet he was with." She rubs her eyes, looking remarkably like Paige when she's exhausted. Overwhelmed. "He got in my face."

"Oh my God. I'm so sorry. We should have gone with you. Beau should have gone."

"It's okay." She hesitates. "Mateo was there."

"Which Mateo?"

Surely not Mateo Garza, A-list movie star and Beau's best friend. Surely not the man who has always been suspicious of Emily. He and Emily don't get along. They bristle in one another's presence. There's an energy between them that seems like it might turn to angry sparks at any moment. Or maybe it's some kind of sexual chemistry.

"Mateo Garza," Emily says.

"He was there? Did you two… did you two have a discussion?" I mean an argument. If Mateo showed up at the wrong time, if he gave her a hard time on her hardest day, I'm going to give him hell. Was he just standing there outside the courthouse?

"He helped me block the reporter. He kept him away from me so I could get to my car." She blushes, the pink strong beneath her pale skin. "Actually, I'm in his debt."

It sounds like there's more she's not saying. Mateo, the hero of the moment.

I guess I'll have to thank him for helping Emily.

Then again, he might not have done her any favors. After all, he's a former hometown boy who became a famous movie star. It will be a bigger story that he was at the courthouse. There's bound to be an article somewhere in the Eben Cape Herald, beneath a feature piece on the blueberry pie competition. Well, let's hope no one actually reads it.

"But you're okay now," I say to reassure her, but it comes out more like a question.

"I'm great." Emily puts her hand on Paige's blonde locks, so much like her own. Love shines in her eyes when she looks at her daughter. "It's time we headed home."

Paige gives me a cheerful wave from her mother's side. "Don't move the pieces."

"I won't." That's our tradition, now that we live apart. Even though my house is on the same cliff, it's not the same as living together. So we leave our Monopoly games open until the next time we see each other. Unfortunately, I'll be starting tomorrow in jail.

Watching them go hand-in-hand squeezes my heart.

Paige is a miniature version of Emily. Both of them are like those expensive dolls that I could never afford as a little girl—with porcelain skin and blue eyes and blonde curls. In a way they seem delicate. Breakable. But I know better. They're both strong.

And brave.

I'm sad to see them go, but I know that I'm luckier than I ever could have imagined. It's a breezy summer in Eben Cape. I have a brand-new house. The only man I could ever want.

Paige laughs as she climbs into the back seat. "She went to jail four times!" I hear her telling Emily. "Can you believe it? The last one she rolled snake eyes."

"I can believe it," answers Emily. She reaches across Paige's body and buckles her seat belt for her. At seven, Paige can do it herself, but she lets Emily do it anyway.

There's comfort in small gestures. Emily missed doing all those things for Paige while they were apart. She won't waste a single chance to do them now.

When Emily pulls away from the house, she rolls down the car windows.

Paige's arm sticks out one window, waving and waving. Emily waves too. I wave back, standing there until they're on the road to their house. There's a little stand of trees along the way. They'll disappear behind it for a few seconds, then pop into view on the other side.

I tip my head back and bask in the day. It's sunny but cool. The ocean is the most soothing noise in the world. It feels like a sign that things will be okay. The trial is going to be tough. There will be hard days, but more importantly, there will be justice.

And everyone is where they're supposed to be.

Including me. For now, at least, I'm in the best place I could be. The new house is a dream come true. I've never lived in a brand-new house before. You wouldn't believe how clean everything is. It all smells new and fresh. There's tons of possibility in it.

Even the possibility to leave.

I open my eyes again and look at the house. What would we do with it if I went away for college? Board it up and leave it sitting here? I don't like the thought of it standing empty. Obviously, houses can't get lonely. But… maybe a person could be lonely on its behalf.

I might feel that way, if we were gone for weeks at a time.

I'd miss the house. I'd miss the view. I'd miss the people most of all.

I never knew having this many choices would feel like this.

For most of my life, I concentrated on one goal. My main plan hasn't changed. I want to graduate from college and become a social worker.

There are many paths to get there, though. Different schools I could choose from.

I feel a bit like I did when I first came to Maine. My clothes were all wrong for the weather.

I didn't fit here. Each of the choices feels like a new climate I'd have to learn.

Part of the complexity comes from the people, too.

Before, it was me and Noah against the world. Now I have Beau, but Paige is very much a part of our lives. Anything I decide will also affect her. I might not be her nanny anymore, but I can't turn off caring about her. I don't want to, anyway.

I'm still thinking about it when I head back inside the house. Our Monopoly game will, of course, be left untouched. My cell phone buzzes on the table next to it. It's ringing.

Beau, maybe.

I turn it over and find an unknown number. I've been talking to a lot of admissions counselors, but I don't recognize this particular area code. "Hello?"

"Jane Mendoza?" A man. I don't recognize his voice.

"This is she."

"This is the Maine Investigator. I know you're close friends and neighbors with Emily Rochester. Do you know about the scene at the courthouse today?"

My heart pounds. Emily hasn't been back from the courthouse very long, so it must be the same guy who accosted her. "Nothing happened at the courthouse today."

"So you do know. Listen, we have it on camera. I'm looking for some insight before we go to print. Get her side of the story on paper. Or maybe your side of the story."

It feels like the walls are closing in on us. On the cliffside. "I don't know what you're talking about," I say over the buzzing of panic in my ears. "Don't call back."

I hang up on him.

It feels very final, even if I'm just tapping a screen.

If no one has anything to say about Emily at the courthouse, this will all pass by quickly. Right? Emily Rochester and Mateo Garza will be a local news story that everyone has forgotten by next week. Except that this guy worked for the Maine Investigator, a larger paper than the one here in Eben Cape. This could be bigger than I feared.

No. No, I'm sure it will blow over. Emily's finished testifying. She's with her daughter. And she lives so close. Close enough for us to keep an eye on her.

My heart keeps racing anyway.

CHAPTER FIVE

Mateo Garza

I T'S FUNNY HOW life keeps circling back to the same things. The same people. I left Eben Cape for Los Angeles, and I still ended up with Beau Rochester as a best friend. Now we're both in Eben Cape again. Beau lives next to the house he grew up in, and I have a small beach house I rented. I think he spends more time talking to Emily Rochester now than he did in school, and that's saying something. Same places. Same people. We both have our own money now, Beau and I, and here we are on a fishing boat.

The boat is an upgrade from the speedboats we used to take out on the water when we were younger. This one has an interior. It has an enclosed wheelhouse so you don't have to feel even a drop of the ocean while you steer. It looks over the bow of the boat, where we are. A couple of rich jackasses who have lost their touch.

"You should find another hobby," I tell Beau. "You're absolutely terrible at this."

He glares at me from his position at the railing. "Compared to what? You don't have a line in the water."

"It's too much fun to watch you." Beau used to attract catches like he was a fish magnet. Today, not a single bite. "You've forgotten all your skills."

He holds up his pole. "This is a fishing pole, Mateo. You hold it in your hands. Is that beyond you?"

"Yes," I tease. "I usually hire someone to fish for me while I watch. You're doing a great job, by the way. You're going to get a huge tip when this is over."

Beau gives a gruff laugh and goes back to staring at the bobber on the end of his line. The joke is that I can afford to pay a person to fish for me while I pretend to be a fish voyeur. So could Beau. We could hire a whole crew. How times have changed.

"Goddamn it," Beau says. "This thing is fucking with me."

"What thing?" I peer over the railing at the bobber. "You're not getting bites. There's nothing down there."

"Mind your own business."

"Why are we out here? We don't need fish to survive. This ship has a couch we could be sitting on."

"Go sit on it, then. I'm going to catch something." He furrows his brow and concentrates. A breeze comes up from the water. The ocean still smells the same. The sun feels the same on my skin. We're the ones who are different now. Eben Cape stayed the same while our lives rearranged themselves like portable sets. He and Paige were trapped together on the island of Coach House. Then Jane came along. And then, to everyone's surprise, Emily Rochester. Now everything's in a new place.

In my opinion, which hasn't been humble for a very long time, Beau Rochester takes things too seriously. I've known him long enough to know he'll never stop. Acceptance is the first step toward being friends with a guy like that. You're not going to change him. You can only watch him try to catch a fish on a nice-as-hell boat.

Prepare to be disappointed, though. He almost never catches anything these days. He's more patient in some ways since he had custody of Paige, but less patient in others. He's always impatient to get back to Jane, for instance. There were times in our past that we'd go out on a Friday night and come back home on a Tuesday. Beau would never agree to be away from Jane that long.

Only way he'd ever do that is if she asked him. I don't think she would.

How long have I been away from Emily? A day? Probably can't count it as "being away" when we're not together. Emily wouldn't want that, anyway.

Unless she would. I've never met a woman more in need of a shoulder to cry on. I wouldn't go so far as to say she needs a partner, though. Emily's tackling her newly resurrected life with grim determination. She's writing that damn memoir with the kind of focus that I think most people would envy. In my business, when someone writes a book, it's cause to throw a party and get drunk on champagne. Emily works on it like she's going into battle.

Worked out for her, though. She got the book deal, though the memoir itself won't be finished for a while. And it won't come out until next year.

This time, Beau doesn't concentrate for as long as I thought he would. After a few minutes he puts the pole in one of the holders on the railing. He stretches his arms over his head.

"I'm going to go down. Do you want anything?"

"Taking a break so soon?"

"Like a beer, asshole. You want a beer?"

"Yes."

Beau goes into the cabin. Three steps down to a nice-sized living room with the previously mentioned couch and a full kitchen behind it. There's also a little bedroom down there. Like I said, not a speedboat.

My phone rings, and I lean against the railing and take the call. It's my agent. Catrina Gonzales is the best in the business. She's small. Physically short, which makes the guys on the other side of the table underestimate her.

"I'm on vacation." I use an exasperated voice. "You know that."

"There's a movie." Catrina isn't the type to get overexcited. Something has her excited now. "They want you. The director of that plane crash movie. This is huge, Mateo."

"I told you. I'm not taking any movies right now."

"Right, right, right. I get it." I can see her in her office in LA, pacing in front of a set of picture windows. "You're on personal leave. Guess what?

Celebrities of your status don't get personal time. A-listers do not take extended vacations. And they're offering big money."

"Gonzales—"

"I'm sending you the script." I can tell she has me on speakerphone now. "They want to move fast, and this is the kind of project you've always wanted."

"It's not a good time to discuss—"

"It's artsy, Mateo. It's not another action flick. This is how you move beyond typecasting. This is how you get to the next level."

"Fine. I'll give it a look." I'm trying to spend an afternoon watching my best friend fuck up the simple act of fishing. Arguing with Catrina doesn't get me closer to that goal. "Email it to me, and I'll let you know what I think."

"You know, Mateo, you've been talking about getting into producing."

The boat rocks over a swell. A cloud passes over the sun. Where is she going with this? "So?"

"So, I didn't know you had a personal relationship with Emily Rochester." Catrina's voice is brimming with possibility and the thrill of having inside knowledge.

"Jesus fucking Christ."

"Imagine. It would be the blockbuster of the

year. Her memoir. Big screen. Mateo Garza, starring and producing. And you know her. Like I said, personal relationship." She emphasizes the *p* sound at the end of *relationship*. "You could bring her on tour. You could interview with her."

A vision of me and Emily sitting on a screen-appropriate couch between fake plants pops into my head. Where is Gonzales getting this idea? "What the hell are you talking about?"

"See? This is the kind of energy you could bring to a major project with Emily. You have the face for it, and you'd be so believable on screen."

I turn away from the cabin like I'm turning away from the crowd at a party. "This isn't an act. What are you talking about?"

She pauses. "You don't know you're on the news right now? CNN has it. It's the top story on BuzzFeed. I think you might trend on Twitter on the East Coast."

Shit. I didn't help Emily get out of the court-house for the headline. I find it completely un-newsworthy that I made some paparazzi back the hell up in my own hometown, for a woman I've known since we were in high school. The world sees it differently. And it's a very different world from the one we grew up in. Social media is like tossing a cigarette into a dried-out forest. You're going to end up with a fire that stretches for thousands of acres.

"You have to shut this down." The sea breeze cools my face. I wish it would cool my racing thoughts, too. "Right now."

My agent laughs. "I can't shut it down."

"You don't understand. That wasn't a publicity stunt. There has to be someone you know who could stop it."

"Mateo, you can't shut it down." She almost sounds sympathetic. "You can only amp it up. Way up. Ride this one all the way to the end. You and Emily could both end up with a nice payday."

"I'm not concerned with the payday," I insist. I know she's used to working with actors who are busy shuffling jobs like cards in a deck, trying to come up with the most cash in their bank accounts. "I don't want it to happen like this."

"It's already happening. Take advantage. This is how you get to the next level, Mateo. You can stop taking those action meathead roles and do something serious for once. And with a producer credit, doors are going to open for you all over Hollywood."

It's like she can't hear a word I'm saying. Acting means being able to shut up when the director yells *cut* and talk when the cameras are rolling. I spend half my time on camera in other places, promoting films or sitting for interviews or pretending to spill my deepest secrets. But now, when it counts, my agent can't hear a goddamn thing.

"So, here's what I think we should do." She starts ticking off a checklist of ways to keep the story alive. The longer it has a beating heart, the longer we have to make a deal. First thing on her list is to appear in public with Emily Rochester. A walk down the main drag in Eben Cape will be enough, if there are photographers. My agent will ensure there are photographers. My entire soul sighs at the thought of staging a PR walk in Eben Cape. This is supposed to be one of the few places on earth that people don't treat me like I've crash-landed from another planet populated only by actors and hot people. They don't have such a sense of urgency about it, like they do in other cities. Better take my picture fast, before I get beamed back to LA. Not in Eben Cape.

Beau comes up from the cabin, two beers in hand. He takes one look at my face and narrows his eyes. He cocks his head. I know he can tell something's wrong. He'll ask me about it the moment I get off the phone. Sooner, if he gets impatient.

I can't listen to another word out of my agent's mouth.

"I have a meeting." I interrupt her mid-stream and shoulder my way into the priority spot in the conversation. "We'll come back to this later. In the meantime, I don't want any press interviews. I'm not talking to anybody about this. I don't care what they pay."

"Mateo," she scolds. This is a familiar scolding. "That's not how you're going to make the—"

Make the connections you need to be at the top of the industry. That's what she was going to say. Catrina has said it before, and I'm sure she'll say it again.

"Everything okay?" Beau asks. It should be okay. We're out on the boat. It's beautiful out on the water. He has beers. It was going to be the perfect day before all this bullshit with the press started.

"We have to get back. Something's wrong."

CHAPTER SIX

Emily Rochester

M Y HANDS ARE blue. I've been baking all morning.

Yesterday we picked blueberries, filling up entire buckets, the same tin buckets that I used when I was a child. They're overflowing with ripe, juicy blueberries. We started with blueberry pancakes, then I made a blueberry crumble.

Now half of the kitchen is covered in flour. We're making muffins.

Paige got distracted. I love leaving the door open. She goes outside to paint her rocks and comes back in to help me mix. Her mouth has turned blue from the blueberries. She loves them fresh, the way a child of Maine should.

Strange, how memories work. Human brains are fallible. I remember picking blueberries with Joe, both of us laughing, happy. Were we really happy? Was he always this way or did he change at some crucial moment? We almost never remember things as they actually happened. Our perceptions are always influenced by the past—things that, by definition, we can only remember. We can never go fully back to the way things were.

I want to create new memories with Paige.

The best ones probably look like something out of a movie, or a children's book. They probably look something like what we're doing right now. I stand at the stove, oven mitt on one hand, watching the timer tick down. The scent of blueberry muffins fills the air. Outside, the world is green and fresh. I always loved summers at Eben Cape. The long days felt so full of possibility.

"Mom," comes a voice. "Mom. Mom. Mom."

That's the way she calls me, repeatedly, and I love it. I'll never get tired of hearing her voice. I put the tray into the oven and step outside.

The glare burns my eyes.

What could be more perfect than this moment? Paige, calling to me to show me something that delights her? I prayed for another moment like this when I was on the run. Now I have it.

"Look at that bird," Paige says, pointing to

the top of a tree. I squint.

There's a mama bird feeding her babies, a little late in the season. Maybe she's like me, late, but trying her best at motherhood. "She's beautiful."

"It's so blue," says Paige. The bird is intensely blue. Brilliant against the blue of the sky. A wisp of a cloud passes behind it, making it stand out even more.

It's hard to take my eyes off Paige to look at the bird. She's growing up so fast. It's a cliché even to think it, but it's true. Her hair is pulled back in a blonde ponytail and she looks gangly in her summer shorts and T-shirt. She's so young, and yet it's a shock to find that she's seven years old and her baby roundness is mostly in my memory now.

"I love that color."

"Me, too," she agrees, tilting her head to the side. I wonder if she's going to draw it later. Another memory. Sketching a bluebird while her mom cooks dinner.

The oven timer goes off, and I return to the kitchen. I grab a potholder and open the oven. But I'm rushing, halfway in a dream, and I touch the inside of my wrist to the 400-degrees-Fahrenheit metal.

It burns, and I jump, letting out a small sound of surprise and pain. I finish pulling out the muffins, set them on a counter, and go to run my hand under the sink. The water burns in a new way. There's already a red mark on my skin, and I know it will leave a scar.

I have lots of scars in places no one sees, places no one will ever see. Those are the scars I didn't give myself and, in a twisted way, that makes this one better. I can hurt myself, but no one will ever be able to hurt me again. That's a promise I made to myself when Rhys died.

I turn around to check on Paige and see my phone blinking. I pick it up. Twenty missed calls? No one calls me. Jane and Beau have my number, but they come over every day, so we usually don't have to call. The prosecutor talks to me, but this isn't her number. These are numbers from all over Maine. There's even one from LA.

I scroll through the missed calls, and then I check my texts.

There's my agent, Amy Martin. She's the one who got me a book deal based on the proposal.

She sent me a single message. It's a link.

I click on it. My screen opens to a national news outlet. There's a picture of me. I'm holding up my hand, trying to shield my face from the camera. It's a little blurry. My hair is in motion, but you can feel my panic through the lens.

The headline is in all caps. MATEO GARZA'S HIDEAWAY BRIDE.

A knot forms in my chest. This is so much more than I thought it would be. National news? I thought we would be in the Eben Cape Herald, circulation a thousand. This is bigger and scarier. Are other people going to pick this up? Based on the missed calls, probably. This could be more than news in a crime column about a dirty cop in a small town in Maine. With Mateo Garza's name attached, it could be massive. It could be an internet sensation. Worse than news, it could be gossip.

Fear squeezes my heart. I need to see Paige. I need to make sure she's okay. To rest my hand on her silky curls. Maybe that feels like overkill—she's not really in danger—but a mother's instinct doesn't listen to logic.

I run to the window and look out.

Panic squeezes my throat. There's Paige standing by the tree, but she's not alone anymore. The bird has flown away, leaving its nest of babies. The man wears a T-shirt and jeans. He could be anyone walking around Eben Cape. A local, though I don't recognize him. A tourist. They love to hike, even though this is a private mountain.

Except he has a camera around his neck, a big, bulky camera with a big lens, the kind that reporters have. No, correction. The kind that paparazzi have.

Paige chatters to him, pointing up at where the bird used to be. She doesn't know anything is wrong. She doesn't know we're under attack.

Then I'm running. Time moves so slowly. It feels like an eternity before I can actually reach her, even though it must be seconds. I'm breathless by the time I push him away from her. He got too close. He has his finger on the button of his camera. How dare he? How dare he speak to a seven-year-old girl? How dare he take a picture of her? How dare he do this just to get a tabloid story?

"Get away from my daughter!"

Paige jerks backward, her eyes wide. I don't blame her. I sound scary, even to myself.

"Not far enough. Back up." My pulse thunders at his audacity. How dare he come into my yard and talk to my daughter? How dare anyone? "Who are you?" I demand.

He doesn't look concerned to see me. In fact, his eyes light up. "Emily Rochester. You're the person I came to see. Would you care to comment on Mateo Garza?"

I step in front of Paige. "No goddamn comment," I say, trembling with adrenaline. I faced my own brother when he wanted to kill me. I faced my husband a hundred times when he was angry, when he lashed out with his fists, when he held me down. I'm not afraid when I'm in danger, but I'm terrified when there's a threat to my daughter. "Get the hell off my property."

He doesn't seem surprised by my animosity. He gives a smile that I think is supposed to be charming. "One little quote," he says. "Have you seen his movies? I can see the appeal. Then again, maybe you're hoping to use him to get your book made into a movie."

I gasp, shocked by the idea, by the accusation, by the balls on this guy. "I'll have you arrested for trespassing. What you're doing is illegal, and I'll see you in jail for it. You don't come near my daughter. You don't come on my property." I left my phone in the house. Even if I wanted to call the police, I couldn't do it. "Turn around and leave. Turn around right now."

Paige shivers behind me. "Mama?"

"Go inside, sweetheart. Now."

She runs away, and I can finally take a deep

breath. At least she's inside the house. But the door is open, and this guy is still on our property. I feel alone and small. No matter how hard I want to be strong, I'm still a woman in a world of angry men.

"I have no comment for you. Leave or I'm calling the cops."

He smiles. "The cops? Are you sure they'd even come? After all, you're Joe Causey's sister, the woman who's trying to put him in jail. And if he goes down, he's definitely going to bring some of his dirty cop buddies with him."

"Good," I say, my voice tight. "Now leave."

"Mateo Garza is a player. He'll take you for a ride. Send the tabloids after you. Then he'll leave. Trust me. I've been following the guy for years."

It's strange. The words shouldn't have any effect on me. I don't have any romantic ideas about Mateo. Even if I did, in the deep-down place where my womanhood can't help but recognize a handsome man, they're only temporary. I would never be with a man like him. In fact, I will never be with a man at all. My safety and my independence mean too much.

"Get out," I tell him. "Don't come back."

He backs up a few steps, but his hands go to the camera. The shutter clicks. This asshole is taking photos of me, and I know what it's going to look like. The same as I did on that news website. Me, hysterical and furious. "See you around, Emily."

Somehow the way he says my name sounds disrespectful. He wanders down the road, which winds down to the bottom of the cliff.

I cross my arms over my stomach and watch him go.

Only when he's out of sight do I return to the house. And lock the door.

The idyllic moment with the kitchen door open and the mama bird feels miles away.

"What was that man talking about Uncle Mateo for?" asks Paige.

Part of me wants to collapse from the pounding fear. And the intense relief of having him gone. But I force myself to present a calm façade for my daughter. "He's not a good man. He's a reporter stirring up trouble. Nothing is happening between me and Uncle Mateo."

I get out plates. I pour glasses of water from the Brita. Paige and I sit down at the table with our muffins. My palms are slick with anxiety. This conversation is going to be a big deal. For me. For Paige. I'd hoped I wouldn't have to have it with her yet.

"Paige, I wanted to tell you about something." I peel the cupcake wrapper off my muffin. "If any man or woman approaches you, and they're a stranger, don't talk to them."

"Is that man coming back?"

"He might. He's not supposed to, but sometimes people do things they aren't supposed to."

"And then they go to jail."

I pause, not sure how to answer. I don't know if she's saying that because of the threat I made to the paparazzi. Or because her uncle is on trial for murder. Or simply because she's used to jail as a regular part of Monopoly. "Sometimes. Sometimes they go to jail."

"Are more people coming?"

"They might."

"Why?"

Paige takes a bite out of the top of her muffin.

In an ideal memory, in an ideal life, I would never have to say these things to my daughter. I would never have to feel this fear. This anger. I would never have to hide it, so she won't be scared. In my ideal memory, it's muffins and blue skies forever.

"Other people know about some of the things that happened with your uncle Joe. They know I'm writing a book about it. It makes them want to take pictures." A stab of regret. "I probably shouldn't be writing it, Paige. I think it was a mistake."

"But you're a writer, Mom." Paige eats another section of the top of her muffin.

"I brought this on us. It's because of my book that they want to know more about us. I shouldn't have done it." That's not exactly true. I know that even as I say it. Joe Causey's trial is naturally public information. A dirty cop who murdered his sister's husband will always be salacious news. And Mateo Garza will always be a topic of interest. This guy even said he's been following him for years. It's more about him than it is about me.

Paige screws up her face and shakes her head. "You said I could do anything. The same way *you* can do anything, like writing a book."

"As a job. That's what I meant. You can choose to be anything you want for a career."

"You didn't say it was just jobs," Paige argues. "You said anything."

How can I have said that to Paige, and meant it, if I can't live that myself? Guilt heats my face. Part of living fearlessly in this new version of myself is that I need to speak my truth. I can no longer be in hiding. Not just physically hiding, but emotionally hiding from what had happened.

I've spent enough time doing that.

Besides, the advance from the memoir paid for Coach House. Beau offered to rebuild and cover everything. I couldn't accept. I didn't want to be controlled by or beholden to a man again. He wouldn't have held it against me, but I didn't want it, down at my core.

I wanted this for myself.

I need to be independent.

Well, now I am. Now I'm alone in Coach House with my daughter while a strange man lurks outside. I haven't gone back to the window to see if he's gone. Part of me doesn't want to. Part of me would rather retreat. Pull down all the shades and pretend we're not home.

But I'm done hiding.

Done.

"What I mean is that we have to be on the lookout for ourselves. I'm always going to protect you the best I can, but there are times you might be alone. I want you to know what to do. You don't have to speak to strangers, even if they ask you questions. You come find me right away. Or someone else you trust."

"Like Uncle Mateo?" she asks.

"Like Uncle Mateo," I agree. "Or Uncle Beau. Or Jane. Your teacher at school. We need to look out for ourselves, and part of that is knowing when to ask for help."

"If someone comes to talk to me, I should ask for help," Paige repeats. She puts her rocks out on the table. Five of them in one fist. "Is that what you do when someone comes to talk to you and you don't know them?"

"Sometimes I do."

Sometimes, like when I came out of the courthouse and let Mateo usher me through that shitshow. But I'm spinning another pleasant memory to Paige. I'm giving her the neat dichotomy of stranger danger vs. safe person. People we know aren't always safe. Rhys was a prime example.

Paige has eaten the entire top of her muffin, leaving the bottom in its wrapper. "Can I have another one?" Her blue eyes light up. My chest unclenches. I go to get Paige a second muffin and peek out into the yard. There's no sign of the reporter anymore. No cars out there, either.

I've been at the mercy of a man before. I've been at the mercy of his money. I won't be at the mercy of this asshole, or anyone else. Asking for help is one thing. Relying on a man for safety and survival? No.

I have to stand on my own. It's the only way I can live.

CHAPTER SEVEN

Mateo Garza

NOT ONLY IS my agent being deliberately stupid about this, not only has my five minutes with Emily Rochester become national news, but they went to her house.

Some asshole went to her house. I pace around the beach house and try not to become a complete madman. It's been, what, two days, and there are people at her house? It's not a matter of shutting it down from LA anymore. The vultures are already here.

Even if I leave, I can't draw them away from her. I was the crack in the door. Emily is the prize. They won't stop until they draw blood.

When I can think straight, I make a call to a friend. Other than Beau, he's the person who could make the most difference in this situation.

Liam North answers on the first ring. "I

didn't think I'd hear from you," he says, sounding half-worried, half-amused. "Aren't you on vacation in the middle of nowhere?"

"Things in Eben Cape got a lot more interesting."

"How? Did a circus come to town?"

"The paparazzi did."

"They always come around when you ask them to visit."

"I didn't ask them." I outline the situation with Emily. He listens. No more jokes when I get to the part about how that jackass went to her house. "I need people out here."

"How many?" There's a quiet scratching in the background. He's taking notes.

"A full team. The biggest team you can put together. I don't want anybody setting foot near her house again. Not even on the access road."

"You think they pose that much of a threat?"

"I don't know. But I'm not going to wait for one of them to cross a line to find out."

In forty-eight hours, Liam North's people descend on Eben Cape. There are more of them than I imagined. So many, in fact, that I think about sending some of them back. Then Liam North explains to me that in order to secure the access road, they needed twice as many people.

He goes through a list of parameters they used to calculate the number of personnel. I stop him when he starts getting into the number of hours on shift vs. percentage of secured area. These guys are clearly professionals worthy of their reputation. They know what they're doing. It's my job to trust them. And to pay the very large bill.

They waste no time blocking off the road and setting up a checkpoint. More guys head back into the area surrounding Coach House. It's an old, sprawling property, stretching down to where Beau and Jane live now. All of it needs to be monitored.

I've always thought it was bullshit that there's only one road leading up to the cliff. If somebody got into an accident, you'd have to drive your car through the ditch or the woods. Now I'm glad it's just the one road.

"Two residences," Liam North says after he sends various groups of serious, muscled men to secure the perimeter. "Three adults, one child."

"They have to be protected," I say. "They're all at risk right now."

I'm not very worried about Beau and Jane, truth be told. Beau has the kind of face that telegraphs his mood. I don't think the reporter that harassed Emily would try the same shit with

Beau. And Beau won't let anything happen to Jane.

But all of them need security. All of them are going to have it.

North's men are busy from the moment their feet hit the ground. They're finding the best surveillance spots. They're setting up cameras. This place is going to be protected within an inch of its life.

It's late when I take two men on the team up to Emily's house. I knock softly on the door. Paige is sleeping. Emily said so when I texted her to say we'd be coming up.

Emily opens the door with a grim expression. She steps back to let the three of us in.

"We'd like to sweep your house for bugs and vulnerabilities, ma'am," the first one says to her.

"Go ahead."

His question is just a formality. Emily didn't argue with me when I told her I'd called Liam North. She didn't want me to pay the whole bill. I said we could settle it later. Safety first.

The two guards split up and start clearing rooms in the house. One goes into the living room. The first thing he does is shut the blinds.

Emily crosses her arms protectively over her chest. "I thought you were securing the whole cliff."

"We are," he answers. "But drones can fly up here. Not much we can do about those until they're in sight."

Emily pales. "I didn't think of drones."

The man finishes his circuit of the living room and goes out to cover the rest of the house.

"Don't beat yourself up about it," I tell Emily. "Drones weren't going to be the first thing on your mind. It's not like when we were kids, and there were just newspapers and spies with magnifying glasses."

Emily doesn't even crack a smile. "They're worried about a drone flying up here and looking in the windows. That's like being hunted, Mateo."

"They're not worried about it. They're prepared for it. The curtains are a preventative measure. If the curtains are down, it won't matter if someone flies a drone up here. But the curtains being down doesn't guarantee that it'll happen."

"I know better than to think there are guarantees." She glances toward the windows like the shadow of a drone will appear outside. That guy could have played it a little cooler. He didn't have to scare the hell out of her this late at night.

The two guys come back down.

"Everything's clear," they tell Emily. "We'll be keeping a perimeter around your house and the road up to the cliff, so you shouldn't have any more problems with trespassing. We're communicating with Mr. Garza. However, if you want to reach us directly, you can call this number. It will ring all the guards closest to you." He hands her a business card. "Any time of day or night."

I know it's his job to be there for Emily at all hours, but *any time of day or night* makes me jealous. It's a stupid kind of jealousy that I immediately stamp out. Jealous of a security guard. It's a new low.

"Thanks, guys," I say pointedly. "We'll talk later."

They go out the door, and Emily's shoulders sag. She pushes her hair back from her face and turns in a slow circle, looking around her living room. "I didn't see anything wrong with it before," she admits. "Now I don't know whether we're just sitting ducks."

"You're not."

"That's what those men say, but men don't always know what they're talking about." Her voice has started to show some strain. Emily's struggling not to get louder. I know how terrible she'd feel if she woke Paige up because of this. She paces to one side of the living room, then comes back.

"Emily."

"What?" Her eyes snap up as if she's surprised to see me.

"Come over here for a minute."

Emily steps over, suspicious. "For what?"

I put my arms around her and hold her close. "I probably don't know what I'm talking about, but you seem pretty freaked out."

"Who wouldn't be freaked out?" She feels small in my arms. Her heart's beating fast. "They came in here talking about drones and perimeters. God knows what else they're doing out there. Makes it seem like everything's going to get so much worse."

"Again, I'm not claiming to be an expert on the subject, but I think the security team is going to stop that from happening."

"Stop things from getting worse?"

"Yes. That's why they're here now instead of later."

Emily sighs, frustrated. "This is not how it was supposed to be." Her tone hints at sadness. A real disappointment. Emily grew up in Eben Cape, too. She probably had some idea that things would be simpler if she moved back. The reality is that life was simpler when she was a kid. Wasn't perfect, but it was less complicated. That had nothing to do with Eben Cape. "I was supposed to be able to handle this on my own."

"You're handling it pretty well," I offer. "You have a house with the best view in town."

Emily laughs. She sounds tired. "What's the use in having a great view if you can't open the curtains?"

With every second that goes by, Emily relaxes a little more into the hug. She puts her arms around my waist and holds me back. It shouldn't feel this good to hold her. Even exercising patience for her feels good. I wish to hell she wasn't so shaken up. I wish to hell that prick hadn't come into her backyard. But when Emily rests her head on my chest and sighs, I stop wishing for anything but this moment.

"Better?" I ask.

"Better than what?"

"Better than before."

Emily thinks about it. "You stopped rubbing my back."

"You didn't say that you liked it," I point out, but it's true, I did stop. I had been running my hands up and down her back. Not sure when I stopped, or why, but I start again. "You have spectacular shoulders, too." I trace a fingertip over the line of her shoulder. Trace the side of her neck.

Emily huffs. Another laugh. "Are you sure you want to do that?"

"Why? Do you bite?"

She tips her face up toward mine.

I should not kiss Emily Rochester. I don't care about Emily Rochester, except in that she and Paige are important to Beau. But, hell, I want to kiss her. Something about being this close feels right. Suspiciously, strangely right. Is it just that I'm keeping her safe? Is that all it is? Is all this trouble making me get attached?

It doesn't matter.

I take her face in my hands and kiss her.

Emily lets me in. It wasn't very long ago that we were circling each other like two rival wolves. I didn't want her to fuck up Beau's life again, and she didn't want me to interfere with getting Paige back. Her soft lips on mine are an outcome I couldn't have guessed if I spent my life trying. Emily puts her arms around my neck, her body pressing against mine, and tastes me like I'm trying to taste her.

"Why are you so good at this?" Emily whispers against my lips.

"Practice," I whisper back.

I feel her frown. "Do you kiss everyone like this when you're acting?"

"Hell, no. They get my stage kiss."

"Show me your stage kiss, then." I don't know whether she's being bold like this to distract from how she can't seem to let go of me, or whether she truly possesses a playful side.

I keep my hands where they are and kiss her the way I'd do it in a local theater production. Glancing. Unsexy. It's meant to be seen from the back row, not to be enjoyed.

"And when I'm in the movies, I count to five."

"What?" Emily's bewildered, but it's better than watching her pace the room, scared out of her mind.

"I count to five. They don't usually use more than a few seconds of any given kiss, so I count to five. Some actresses are decent kissers, but if it goes on for too long, it starts to become unbearably strange."

"Stranger than pretending to be another person for a job?"

"Yes. Much."

Emily looks into my eyes. The lamplight in her living room illuminates the wariness in her eyes. This isn't how her life is, in general. She doesn't let me stand in her living room and hug her. She doesn't let me protect her. She doesn't let anyone do anything, since Rhys.

A minute or two of silence passes.

"Show me the real version again," she demands. I've accepted the sensation of holding her. Accepted how it feels when she breathes. I know those patterns. It's the rhythm of a person who has recently been afraid, and who's not anymore.

Don't catch feelings for Emily Rochester, a voice in my head warns. She should be equally wary. It's not good to get attached to a movie star.

We're not bad people, but we can't stay in one place too long. Production happens all over the world. The schedule is hell, if you're good enough. You have to be willing to risk your family to succeed.

That's not an exaggeration. I've seen more than one marriage crumble under the stress of a demanding shooting schedule. I don't want that for Emily.

What I do want is to make her wish come true. I pull her in again and kiss her like she's the only woman I've ever wanted.

CHAPTER EIGHT

Beau Rochester

S UNLIGHT BREAKS ACROSS a large clock tower. It dominates the campus, overlooking miles of buildings, libraries, and dorms.

Students mill around, carrying backpacks and joking with friends. The sound of laughter fills the large, stately courtyard. It's a busy day here. The campus tours have drawn a large crowd.

They're not only recruiting prospective students to the college. There are also booths set up for sororities and fraternities, for clubs, and even for specific majors. All of them vying for the attention of excited young minds. It's a stark reminder of just how much older I am than Jane.

She belongs here.

I don't. If anything, I could be a guest lecturer in the Business Department.

Guilt gnaws at my stomach. Guilt that I'm

taking advantage of a woman too young for me, that I'm drawing her into my life instead of letting her be a carefree college student. I know she wants to be with me. She wants to stay near Paige, but what if she didn't? What if I'd never hired her to be my nanny? If I'd never told her to rub herself off against my shoe? If I'd never defiled her? She'd be like these laughing girls, gathered on stairs and around picnic tables, walking in groups.

Friends. They have friends here. And even if they don't, they're standing at the booths, making friends. Jane isn't doing that. She didn't even want to come. She didn't even tell me about the campus tours. I found out when I saw a flyer in the mail.

"Why wouldn't you go?" I asked her.

"Because it doesn't matter," she'd answered. "Whether the campus is nice or not. I'm sure it is nice, but it doesn't matter. I'm going for the degree. For what I'll learn and for what I'll be able to do with that information. It doesn't matter what the food hall looks like, because I'm never going to go." But that's only because of me. She would have gone to in-person classes. She probably would have stayed in a dorm with a bunch of other teenage kids just like her. I'm the one keeping her from that life. I'm the one holding her back.

My phone buzzes. I pull it out. It's Mateo. He sent me a video. I hit play and it opens up to a news channel.

"Good evening. Channel Nine's Nightly News is pleased to present an exclusive interview with former detective, Joe Causey, who stands accused of murder. We are going to bring an exclusive interview from the Maine County Jail tonight at nine p.m." The clip ends with footage of him walking into one of his trial sessions, wearing a suit and looking... well, official. I know what a snake he is, but then I've always known what a snake he is, even back when I dated his sister. The truth is, he cleans up nice. There's a reason why he got away with being a dirty cop for so long.

Anger runs through my veins. I'm sure they're paying him a pretty penny for this interview, which is much needed, since he's got a fancy defense lawyer and his funds are frozen.

Everything he owns has been confiscated, waiting for the result of the trial.

Joe Causey killed my brother. He hurt Emily Rochester.

And because of him, Paige had to be without her mother for months, believing she was dead.

That alone would be enough for me to hate the man, but he also threatened Jane.

He knows she's important to me. He's willing to use her to hurt me. The thought is strong enough that I want to stride into that tall, white brick building and find her, drag her out of her meeting with the admissions counselor and hold her until I can stop this hollow fear inside me.

But I don't. I continue to lounge against the tree, pretending not to notice when girls give me furtive looks, when they point at me and then giggle with their friends. I suppose some guys would be flattered. Some guys might even see it as an opportunity, a quick fuck with a beautiful young girl. I don't want that. And the only thing it makes me feel is guilt because I did use Jane. I'm still using her, if I'm honest.

I text Mateo.

"Are you watching the girls?"

"Yes," comes the answer right away.

He knows what I mean. The girls are Emily and Paige.

Mateo never got along with Emily, but I still trust him to look after her. And he's like an uncle to Paige.

With the college tour ending late in the day, we're going to be out of town until tomorrow. At least Mateo's there to make sure they're okay, to make sure the paparazzi don't get too close to them.

That's part of why I'm here. I would've wanted to come with Jane anyway, on her tour, as moral support, but I'm also here to make sure the paparazzi don't mess with her.

I have no problems introducing them to my fist.

Sunlight glints off glass as the large doors open and Jane emerges. She's wearing jeans and tennis shoes, a plain T-shirt and a light jacket. Her hair is down, loose in the wind. It's a casual look, but one that takes my breath away. She's beautiful. Seeing her again, even after only thirty minutes, makes my heart squeeze with happiness and with fear. I don't want to hurt her.

A black woman follows her out. I remember her as the advisor who welcomed her. They cross over to me and the woman introduces herself. "Mary," she says, smiling. "And you must be Beau Rochester."

I give a firm handshake. "Nice to meet you."

She's an older woman. I wonder if she's judging me. If she knows how wrong it is for a man with my age and my power and my will to be with a woman like Jane.

There's wisdom in her eyes, though no censure.

"She's told me a lot about you," Mary says. "I understand that you're supportive of her goals. That you talked her into coming to the campus tour."

I make a short, affirmative sound.

Jane gives me a curious look. I'm usually not so surly with someone who's being nice, but I can't help it. Being here makes me restless.

Being on a campus that just emphasizes my wrongness to Jane.

Being out in public where paparazzi could confront her at any moment.

Being faced with this woman, this advisor, who doesn't really know Jane, but in some ways is in a position to take her away from me.

Mary nods. "I'm glad she could come. She would definitely flourish if she lived here in one of the dorms with easy access to the other students, to the study groups, to the professors."

"Oh, no," Jane says. She sounds a little shy but still resolved. "I'm definitely still interested in the correspondence courses. I prefer it that way."

Mary smiles. "That will be a loss to our classrooms, but I understand you have to do what's right for you." They say their goodbyes. I nod to the advisor, who walks away.

Jane looks at me, her expression worried. "Are you okay?"

I ignore the question and point instead to the booths. "Do you want to look around?"

Her dark eyes take in the bustle. "No. Mary gave me the date and time for a meetup with other prospective students who hadn't made a final decision yet, but..." Jane blushes. "People who she thought were passionate about their education. But maybe we can walk along the path. There're so many trees here. And old stately buildings. Just imagine everyone who's learned here over the decades."

I take her hand and we turn down a wide cobblestone path, dappled with sunlight streaming through the trees. As we leave the courtyard, things become quiet. Buildings surround us.

This is where her classes would be if she came to campus. They're empty now. School is on break.

She's the one who reaches for my hand. Usually, I can't stop touching her. I can't stop holding her hand, her waist, her shoulder. I can't stop feeling her smooth skin, but it burns now when she reaches for me. I have to grit my teeth in order to keep holding her hand.

Guilt, that's what this feeling is.

We walk in silence for five minutes. Ten.

Squirrels wander around the lawn, clearly used to humans. They look at us, interested, hoping we might have a pizza crust to throw their way. The buildings feature architecture from every decade.

"You should come here," I tell her.

"I know," she says, her voice animated. "I'm really leaning toward this place. I mean, the school in Connecticut had such a strong social services program, but I really feel like there's something about this one that clicks with me. It's smaller, but there's also going to be more opportunities."

"No," I say. "I mean, you shouldn't do the correspondence courses. You should come here. You should stay on campus."

Her expression falls. "Beau, we've been over this."

"And I'm going over it again," I tell her. "And again, until you do what's right for you, instead of what I want."

She stops on the path and faces me. "What about what I want?"

And then I can't resist any longer. I touch the soft, tender flesh of her neck and then reach around behind to pull her close. "You're too young to know what you want," I tell her. "How do you know you don't want some frat boy or some brooding artist? You don't know. You can't, not until you actually experience this the right way."

"The right way?" she says, scoffing. "What is the right way?"

"Like everyone else," I tell her. "You deserve to have this, like everyone else."

She feels so good against my body. I pull her close and kiss her.

It's a direct denial of every word I've been saying.

The way that I kiss her is full of possession. My words tell her to leave, but my hands pull her close. My words push her away, but my mouth tells her she's mine.

I slide my tongue against hers in sensual demand.

And she moans into my mouth. *Anywhere, anywhere.* I can have her anywhere, that's what she's telling me, but it feels manipulative. God, I'm a selfish bastard.

I want to take her into a classroom and bend her over the teacher's desk. I want to spank her until her ass is red. And then I want to fuck her. It would be a game between us, a game where I'm the professor and she's the student. A game where I have all the power and she bends to my will.

Except the secret is that it's not a game, that the power imbalance between us can never really be overcome. That every time I touch her, I'm hurting her.

Whether she knows it or not.

When I pull away, we're both breathing hard.

I rest my forehead against hers. "She thought you should come to campus," I say, referring to Mary.

I'm guessing that's why Mary told me about it, why she walked Jane out. So that I could help convince Jane to do this. The college advisor knows what's best for her.

And the truth is I know what's best for her too, and it's not me.

"Don't," she says.

"Don't what? Don't point out how much you'll be missing? How much you'll be giving up? Is this really even your dream anymore? Is this your goal if it's changed so much? You wanted to graduate college, Jane. You wanted to go to college, not read a book hours away. Not submit your work online. That wasn't your dream."

"Dreams change," she says.

And I know what she means, that it's allowed

to look different. But I think of something else. Because dreams change in bad ways. They fade. They become overshadowed by lust, by rich men who want a beautiful woman in their bed. "That's what I'm worried about."

CHAPTER NINE

Jane Mendoza

STICKY. THAT'S MY first thought about the pub in the college town. We stayed in a nice hotel. I suggested we could just eat at the nice restaurant downstairs. Beau is the one who insisted that we venture out toward the campus. He's determined that I should experience this.

And though I'm loathe to admit it to him, the truth is I'm curious about it.

So far though, my impression is only that it's loud and crowded and sticky. The tables, the chairs, the floors. The bottoms of my tennis shoes stick to the floors when I walk. We manage to find a high-top table and two chairs. There are two draft beers in front of us. The waitress sails over to us, probably sensing that Beau will tip better than the average college kid.

"What are you getting?" She pulls out a notepad and pen.

"A burger," Beau says.

I'm still studying the sticky plastic menu. "I'll have a Caesar salad," I say, "Thank you."

"No problem," she says to me, taking the menus. Before she slides away, I catch her wink at Beau. Is she flirting with him? It makes me feel strangely possessive.

I never thought I would be the jealous type, but the truth is, Beau looks handsome. He's always been a good-looking man, but compared to all these college boys, the difference is even more striking.

"I'm going to the restroom," Beau says, but he doesn't immediately leave. He waits, watching for my agreement. It's more than permission. He wants to know that I'll be safe here. He may think I don't notice, but he's on the lookout for paparazzi. Thankfully, they don't seem to have gotten wind of this college tour. I give him a broad smile, that's only a little bit fake.

"Of course. I'm fine. Go ahead." He leaves, and then I'm left alone.

The pub seems different without him. Emptier, scarier.

This is how it would've felt if I had come to the college tour without him or without anyone.

Alone. I take a drink from the amber beer bottle and then make a face into my hand. I don't like the taste of beer, I'm discovering. I consider taking out my phone so I can scroll Instagram, anything to distract myself from how out of place I feel. But I don't want to do that.

The truth is, I want to experience this. The secret truth is, I'd like to make friends here, but I don't know how to do that.

The door opens and four boys stumble in.

They've obviously been drinking before they even reached the pub. They're laughing too loud, smiling too hard. The pub is full. Every stool at the bar is taken. The booths are full of people. Too many students crammed together in leather booths.

Maybe that's why they zero in on me.

A single person at a table, an empty chair across from me. They swagger over, and my eyes widen. A guy who seems to be the leader slides into the chair across from me. Beau's chair.

"Hey, sweetheart," he says with a wink.

"Oh," I say, feeling unsure. "Someone's sitting there."

He winks, "I'm sitting here."

My cheeks feel warm, "I'm sorry, but this table is already taken."

Not breaking eye contact with me, he picks up Beau's beer and takes a long swig. "If your date left you alone, that's his problem and my gain. What's your name, sweetheart?"

I glance over at the bartender, but he's busy pouring drinks. The waitress is nowhere in sight. I'm not sure what I'm supposed to do in this situation. I don't really want him sitting here, but I also don't want to make a scene.

His three friends crowd around the table. They don't have seats, but that doesn't seem to bother them. They rest their elbows on the table. One of them comes close to me and slings his arm across the chair that I'm sitting in.

It's too close for comfort. My personal space.

Every muscle in my body tightens.

I don't like when strange men are close to me.

You didn't feel that about Beau, says a small voice in my head, and that's true enough. He made me nervous for completely different reasons than these guys.

"I'm Brandon," the lead guy says when I don't provide my name. "Chemical engineering. My dad's got a job waiting for me at a big oil company, which means I'm not worried about my grades. The only thing I need to do is spend the next four years having the time of my life."

I know better than to respond to him. He's trolling me. Even if he's also telling the truth, he wants a reaction. And unfortunately, I give it to him. "What a waste. Do you know some people would kill for your chance to attend college?"

He grins. "I know, I know. I'm a lucky bastard."

I shake my head. As annoying as he is, there is something actually charming about his oversized confidence. I find myself reluctantly amused. "Well, I can only hope that the chemical engineering professors make your life hell."

He leans forward. Challenge bright in his eyes. "Maybe you can make my life hell, sweetheart. I have an opening for a girlfriend and it looks like you have an opening for a boyfriend."

"She doesn't," comes a low voice. Beau strides up to the table. He doesn't pause.

He's taller than Brandon, wider, stronger, but I'm not sure that's really why Brandon scoots off the chair. It's more about the fierceness of his expression, the certainty that he would win in a fight, even with Brandon's friends to help him.

Beau takes his seat with ease, a look of warning for each of the guys. "She's taken," he says. "Now get the hell away from her."

The other guys scatter faster than I can blink.

Brandon gives Beau a fake salute before heading out. I watch them jostle people at the bar, muscling other guys out of their way.

Bullies, basically. That's what they are.

"Sorry about that," Beau says. "I shouldn't have left you."

"I handled myself," I tell him. "But you don't want to drink out of that beer bottle." I slide over mine. "You can have this one. I can't stand the taste."

The corner of his mouth flicks up. "I have no doubt that you can handle yourself, but you shouldn't have to."

"Because I have you to protect me? I should be able to protect myself. You can't be around me every second of every day."

"Can't I?" he asks as if it was a challenge I threw down.

"No," I say. "You can't. I'm not going to go to in-person classes. I'm going to do correspond-ence classes, but even so I'll have to come here sometimes for meetings, for labs, for study groups. And you can't follow me around as if you don't trust me."

"I trust you," he says. "It's the rest of the world I don't trust." There are TVs above the bar and stationed around the pub. Most of them are playing sports games. One of them catches my eye. It's a news segment and there is a photo of Joe Causey in his old police uniform, smiling, several years younger. My blood freezes. Beau catches my reaction and turns to look. His expression grows grim. "I have to tell you something. He's doing an interview."

"A what?"

"A live interview. Tomorrow night. We're not going to watch it. He's just going to talk bullshit." Panic clenches every muscle in my body. This is much more serious than a group of unruly frat boys. Much more dangerous.

"How is that possible? He's in jail."

"He's doing the interview from there. It's probably just for the money or to try to get public opinion on his side, but it doesn't matter. The only thing that matters is that he broke the law and he's going to jail."

It's not cold in the pub. It's warm. But I find myself shivering. "You don't know that."

"I do," he says.

I know he believes that. There is good evidence against Joe Causey. And Beau's been supplementing the meager budget of the attorney's office to pay for all the lab tests to go through in a timely manner so they'll be well-armed against the smarmy defense attorney that Causey hired, but anything is possible.

Causey was a dirty cop, which means there can be dirty judges.

It means he can bribe the jury.

"Anything can happen," I tell Beau. "I won't feel safe until the verdict is in."

His voice drops low enough that I can barely hear him. But the meaning comes through loud and clear. "If Joe is acquitted, he won't come near you again."

It's not even a promise of protection, those words. Not even an assurance that he'll follow me around campus, the way he's trying to protect me from the paparazzi.

No, he's promising something much more serious, much more permanent. He's promising murder.

If the law doesn't take care of Joe Causey, he will.

In a way, I couldn't even blame him. After all, the man killed Beau's brother. He has a right to take revenge, at least along some lines of thinking, but I can't stand the thought of him doing that.

"Don't," I say.

"Don't what? Don't make the paparazzi leave you alone? Don't tell the frat boys to fuck off?

Don't protect you? You can't ask that of me, Jane. You are mine to hold, to fuck, and to protect."

I shiver again, but for a different reason. The intense possession in his voice should scare me.

And it does, but it also turns me on.

CHAPTER TEN

Emily Rochester

MATEO GARZA STANDS in my kitchen, leaning against the countertop when I come downstairs from putting Paige to bed. He watches in silence while I pour two glasses of wine.

Independent or not, I didn't want to watch Joe's interview alone.

Somehow Mateo makes sense as the person who's going to be here with me. He was there at the courthouse and the beach afterward. He showed up at my door with the security team. I can't stop thinking of the way he kissed me.

That last part has nothing to do with the interview. It's just true.

"Wine," I say. "Cheese." I pull out the pre-cut slices of cheese from the fridge, ready on their little tray. "Crackers. Want anything else?"

"You don't have to watch, you know."

The suggestion in his voice is seductive. *Forget about Joe*, it says. *Forget about the pain he caused you. Forget about Rhys. Forget, forget, forget.* Impossible to do when I'm writing a memoir about him. Then again, I couldn't forget if I wanted to. I have nightmares every night.

"I do have to watch."

Mateo straightens up, his brow furrowed. "Why?"

He and Beau are best friends, but they're very different men. Beau would ask me why I wanted to watch in a broody, frustrated tone. Mateo's holds only curiosity tempered with concern. I'm sure both of them would say that they don't want me to get hurt. It's a noble thing to want.

But hiding from something doesn't make it hurt less. Pretending that Joe never existed won't change the fact that he does. It won't undo what he did.

"Because I still love him. He's still my brother. And family is complicated." I brace for more back-and-forth, more argument about how I shouldn't care about Joe.

Instead, Mateo picks up the cheese tray and the box of crackers. "You can't blame me if I eat the whole thing."

"You're going to eat an entire box of crackers during the interview?"

"I'm not planning on it," he says with a smile. "I'm just saying that if it happens, it's only because I really, really like these crackers."

We settle on the living room couch. I have a flash of dread. I got the wine and the cheese and the crackers so I'd have something to do during the interview. Counter it with decent wine and melt-in-your-mouth crackers. What if this is just another attempt to hide? If I sip wine and eat cheese, am I pretending this isn't a big deal?

No. It is a big deal, otherwise I'd turn it on in the background while I cleaned, like some shitty reality show. Mateo came over for moral support. A little light alcohol isn't a hiding place.

We're too early for the interview and end up having to watch the commercials. A flashy BMW hurtles down a mountain road. A woman in a gown with a plunging neckline rapturously sprays perfume. A car dealership in the next town shouts at us about zero-percent down.

"Emily."

"Yeah?"

"You need more wine?"

I look down and discover the glass is half-empty. "I can get it."

Mateo plucks my glass out of my hand and goes into the kitchen as the news anchor starts the program. Her eyes are bright as she describes some of the worst moments of my life like they're splashy headlines. They are splashy headlines now, I suppose. I contributed to that by getting a book deal. But I refuse to feel guilty about that now. It was Rhys's choice to be who he was. It was Joe's choice to do what he did. I'm just writing about what happened to me as a result.

"Is he on yet?" Mateo returns to the living room and hands me my glass. He sits a little closer this time.

"Not yet." A picture of my book cover flashes up on the screen behind the anchor. B-roll footage of me exiting the courthouse, partially blocked from view by Mateo. His handsome, smiling headshot. "They're acting like you're already in the Lifetime movie."

Mateo shifts on the couch next to me. "I would never be in a Lifetime movie about all this. It deserves only the best studio. HBO at the bare minimum."

I laugh at his joke, but it doesn't sound real. It doesn't feel real. Because they're switching over to the main event—Joe's interview.

He's dressed in his prison uniform, a dull

green color with a white T-shirt underneath. The film crew has been fairly skillful at disguising that they filmed the interview in one of the jail's meeting rooms. The space falls into shadow behind Joe. Why did they go through all that trouble with the lighting? The uniform is a dead giveaway.

I'm distracting myself with it. They're done with the pleasantries. My brother frowns as the interviewer, one of the high-powered names from the station, asks him to go back and describe his childhood.

"It wasn't a good situation," Joe says, after a weighty pause. "My father wasn't a good parent."

"Can you say more about that?"

"He was abusive. He'd beat us every night. The only escape we had was school."

"When you say we, you mean your sister."

"Yes, my sister Emily." Joe clears his throat like he's getting choked up. He wasn't in tears the night he murdered Rhys. His eyes were dry and bright. That's because he wasn't going to stop with my husband. "I tried to protect her, but I was still a child. We suffered for years."

"Don't crush it," Mateo says.

"What are you talking about?"

"Your wine glass." I'm holding it so tightly

my knuckles are white. "A cut on your palm would make life miserable."

I put the glass down on the coffee table, frustration beating at my chest. Joe is still going on about our father on the screen. "He's saying all this like it was an excuse. He's putting words in my mouth."

Mateo studies me. "Your dad was an asshole, though."

"*We suffered for years.* He makes it sound like every second was horrible. I'm not defending him. Our father. He was a terrible parent. But I didn't go out and murder anyone because of it. I wish Joe would get my name out of his mouth."

This, most of all. I didn't want to hide from the world anymore. That's why I started writing my memoir. I also didn't want to be exploited. I wanted to choose which parts of my past to grapple with. I've already grappled with the fact that my father wasn't a good man. Joe is dredging all this up again to make himself look like a victim in the present. It's disgusting.

"I wish that for you, too," Mateo says.

It quiets some of my ferocious anger. I didn't know until Mateo said it that it was one of the only things I wanted to hear from another person. *I'm sorry* sounds like trite bullshit at this point. I'd be fine if no one ever said *it could be worse* again in my lifetime.

I take a sip from my wine without crushing the glass. "Thank you," I say, with its sweetness still on my tongue. "For saying that."

Mateo pats my shoulder. We keep watching.

It gets worse.

"I can't help but think that's why my sister was attracted to Rhys Rochester. There was nothing I could do to stop her from getting married, but—" He swallows hard, putting on an angry, disappointed expression. "I'm her older brother." A hand to his chest. "How many years was I supposed to stand by and watch him beat the pulp out of her?" Joe's voice rises. "How could anyone blame me—"

"I understand," says the interviewer. "It's obviously an emotional topic."

"I'm sorry," says Joe.

"That's okay." A compassionate pause from the interviewer. "So… you felt you had to take action."

"I saved her the only way I could. Rhys Rochester was never going to stop hurting her until he was dead."

"You killed him to save your sister's life."

"Yes." The anger melts away from Joe's face.

He could have been an actor. Maybe he should have been. His posture shifts until he looks forlorn. Despairing. "I know it was against the law. I'm a cop." A bitter laugh. "I was a cop. I was sworn to uphold the law, but I couldn't let a monster roam the streets of my small town. I couldn't let him hurt my little sister for one more day."

I notice the heat of my tears first. Then the sting. Mateo reaches for the remote and turns off the TV.

He takes the glass back out of my hand and puts his arm around me, curling me close to his side. "What a bastard," he says. He's pissed.

"Is it weird—" My sobs feel compressed into my lungs somehow. They don't want to come out. I don't want this emotion on display, but I can't help it. That night on the boat wasn't about saving me at all. It was about getting me out of the way. "Is it weird that I wish that was how it really happened?"

"No," Mateo says. "No, it's not." Gentle fingers on my jaw turn my head.

He kisses me through my tears, and then he kisses them away. Every drop of salt disappears under his attention. Mateo kisses me with such pure patience. I could almost believe it would be okay if I cried forever. He'd just keep tending to my tears. *This is not independent,* a judgmental voice whispers. I ignore it. I want more of him. I put my arms around his neck and kiss him back, and he's there, waiting. His hands trace a path near my spine. Too much heat in the room to cry anymore.

"Come to Paris," he murmurs against my mouth.

I resurface with a confused blink. "What?"

"Come to Paris with me. We can fly there tonight and be back in a couple of days. We'll take my private jet. It will get your mind off things. And make it harder for the paps to find you."

A laugh bubbles out. "What? No."

"Why not?" His dark eyes glint with challenge.

"For lots of reasons."

"Name one."

"The fact that you hate me, for one thing." The words spill out of my mouth before I can stop them. I didn't mean to expose my thoughts that way. Or the hurt that slips into my voice.

"I don't hate you. I didn't know if I could trust you. And maybe… maybe I'm an asshole."

"Meaning what?"

"Meaning maybe I didn't like the way you picked Beau in high school. The way you picked him without giving me a second glance. It was immature."

"And now you're mature?"

"I wouldn't go that far, but I want to take you to Paris anyway. Let me."

"What about Paige?"

"She could stay with Beau and Jane. She loves staying with them."

"I already feel like a terrible mother." A piece of my heart will always be bruised by the things I had to do to protect myself. It's true that she loves her nights with Beau and Jane, but there's absolutely no way I'm taking a vacation without her. "I can't abandon her again. I won't."

Mateo shakes his head. "If you could only see yourself the way I see you. You're a great mother, Emily. The best. You sacrificed so much for her. Not only after Rhys died. I know you protected her before then."

I know. He wasn't there, but he knows. I did protect her. I wished, desperately, that I had a mom to do the same thing for me when I was a kid. I wished, desperately, that I didn't have to become the mom I never had because of Rhys. But I did, and I would do it again. I would do it all over again for Paige.

"Let's take Paige to Paris, then."

I pull back so I can see his eyes. He's serious. "She's not even your child."

"Listen, I love Paige. And I think she'd have a great time. More importantly, so would you." No one has a more charming grin than Mateo. It's full force now, overwhelming for how handsome it is. His eyes sparkle. "Actually, the most important thing is that I'd have a good time."

"She's seven," I argue, though my heart has already accepted the invitation. Hope rises like champagne bubbles. "What is she supposed to do in Paris?"

"Emily." A serious expression, this one so playful I almost laugh out loud. "You must know about Disneyland Paris."

"Just—to be completely clear." Mateo still has his arms around me, big hands on my back. It's the steadiest I've felt since the courthouse, except for the few occasions when we hugged. When we kissed. "You want to fly to Paris on a private jet, with no notice, to take my child to Disney World."

"Disneyland Paris," he corrects. "And I told you. I want to take myself."

"What do you like to do at Disneyland Paris?"

"Obviously, ride Big Thunder Mountain over and over again. It's far superior to the one in Orlando." Mateo stands up from the couch and offers me his hand. "Come on. It's summer. Paige doesn't have school. The paparazzi are going to continue to be insane. Let's go somewhere else."

CHAPTER ELEVEN

Mateo Garza

I MIGHT HAVE been too ambitious with my plan to leave for Paris immediately. We decide to delay until the next afternoon instead of waking Paige up in the middle of the night. It does make things easier when you give people a few hours' notice. Plus, there are a few things I need to pick up before we leave.

Emily has packed the same rolling suitcase three times when I stick my head into her bedroom. "Need anything from town? I'm heading in. Shouldn't take more than an hour."

"I don't think so. I've got a couple of summer outfits packed. Unless there's a secret list that I don't know about."

"There's no secret list."

She glances down at the suitcase. "Just an hour, right?"

"Unless you don't want me to go at all," I offer. "The private jet can still take off if I don't run a couple of errands." This place is surrounded with security. Liam North sends me regular updates about how absolutely nothing is happening. A couple of paparazzi tried to come through a patch of woodland at the opposite side of the property, but they didn't get within sight of the house. The rest of them don't seem inclined to keep trying. Not with armed professionals patrolling the border.

"No," Emily says. "That's fine. I just wanted to be sure—" A light laugh. This one sounds very close to genuine. It sounds like she might be excited about the trip. "I wanted to be sure we wouldn't miss the plane."

"The plane leaves when we're ready."

"I know," she says. Emily flew to Houston on a private jet to find Jane, and that's how they came back to Eben Cape. Things were tense between me and Emily after her arrival. Now, an hour away from her feels like too long.

Maybe this isn't about the schedule at all. But it can't be about me. Can it?

"An hour," I promise. "And then we'll head out."

"Okay." She pushes a lock of hair away from

her face. "Paige, honey. Come have a bath."

"It's too early," Paige calls back from her bedroom. "I have a bath at night." Emily's daughter appears at her bedroom doors, several rocks in one hand and a marker in the other. "It's not night yet."

"It's not going to get dark until late," Emily agrees. "But we're having an early bath today."

I head out to the sounds of Emily negotiating the time of the bath and Paige giving in. Beau's house is my first stop. Takes almost no time to get there in my car. Beau's out on the front porch when I pull in, a glass of iced tea in his hand.

"How's Emily?" he says as I get out of the car.

"Good. We're heading out for a couple of days."

He raises one eyebrow. "Heading out?"

"To Paris. We're taking Paige to Disneyland."

"You know, they have one of those here, in the U.S."

"Two, actually, but that didn't seem far enough from all the nonsense happening in town."

Beau's dark eyes grow suspicious. I bet he's worried for Jane. If I'm skipping town to go to Paris, why should he stick around? "You think something's going to happen?"

"I think she hasn't taken a real vacation in years, and Paige could stand to meet Mickey Mouse. We'll be back before you know we're gone."

He rolls his eyes. "You just came here to tell me you're leaving."

"Yeah, and to tell you that the security's staying. Some of them will travel with us, but I want her house to be secured while we're gone. And yours."

Beau takes a drink of his iced tea. "Why don't you just admit it?"

"Admit what?"

"That you've got it bad for Emily."

"Please."

"A whirlwind trip to Paris? A hundred security guards to keep her safe at night? Are you hoping to put a ring on her finger?"

"Would you care if I did?" I mean for it to sound like a joke, but it doesn't. It sounds like a serious question.

"Are you out of your mind?"

"For suggesting it?"

"I'm with Jane," he says, blunt and gruff, the way he has been since I first met him. "She's the love of my life. Christ. I don't have any weird attachments about Emily. Just don't want her to marry some ridiculous prick who's going to make her life harder."

"Oh. I won't ask her, then."

Beau makes a sound that I recognize as a laugh. "Are you leaving now?"

"In about an hour."

He waves me off. "Get out of here, then. Everything will be here when you get back."

I drive into Eben Cape with his words ringing in my ears. It's my main goal not to make Emily's life harder. And as much as I love to kiss her, we're nowhere near anything like an engagement. But if I did get engaged to Emily, I'd want it to be private. None of that dinner proposal bullshit. People always think it'll be better in front of a crowd, but that's a fantasy for the movies. Popping a high-stakes question in view of a bunch of strangers is a great way for the whole thing to backfire. No. I'd do it outside in her yard, where we could see the ocean. Some quiet night. Just the two of us. Moonlight, maybe.

Second stop after Beau's is the rented beach house. I throw some clothes into a bag. A few years back I worked with a stylist who was a big fan of the "capsule wardrobe." It basically means that all my clothes go with one another. Packing takes less time. I could hire a person to do it, but that seems over the top. Anyway, I have plenty to get through a couple days away from Eben Cape. Anything else we need, we can buy when we get there.

The last stop is a toy store in downtown Eben Cape. I park in one of the public lots around the corner and wait a few minutes to see if the paparazzi have staked out this part of town. Nobody's in sight. A lady walking her dog goes past on the phone. A guy with a stroller heads in the direction of the playground. He's talking to the little one in the stroller. Doesn't look bored, or like he wishes he could be somewhere else.

I get out and head around to the store. A bell tinkles against the glass. Cool air engulfs me.

"Hi there." A dark-haired woman behind the counter greets me with a broad smile. "Are you looking for anything in particular today?"

"I need your Disney shelf." I return her smile, thinking of the dad with the stroller. Does he ever stop in here and pick something up on the way to the playground? I think I'd be a goner the first time my kid poked a chubby hand out of the stroller at a toy in the window. Not that it's a scenario that's ever going to happen.

"Right around here."

"Oh, good. You've got ears." I pick up a

headband with classic Mickey ears, then put it back and choose one with a little Minnie bow in the center. I go with a medium-sized Mickey plush and take them back to the counter.

"Your daughter is one lucky little girl," she says as she rings them up.

My brain freezes. Paige isn't my daughter, but I want to agree with this woman. I want to say *yes, she is* because it would feel good. Both to have a daughter and that some random stranger would think that daughter was lucky to have me. What? No. I've never been the type to fantasize about family life. I know better than to think it's all warm and fuzzy all the time. It's not, even when you're trying your hardest.

It might be simpler to lie, to go along with this, but that's not a good option, either. Eben Cape is small enough that what I said might get around. If it got to the paparazzi—

"My niece," I say, a beat too late.

The woman behind the counter hasn't noticed. She's tucking the ears and the Mickey plush into a paper bag with the store's logo. "So sweet," she says. "She'll love these. On your card?"

"This is the one." I hand it over and chitchat with her while she runs the card and I sign the slip.

"Have a great day," she calls to me as I'm stepping out onto the sidewalk. I wave at her through the window and go back to my car. No paparazzi. Still, I'm tense driving through town. The security guys at the station wave me through.

The bag sits on the passenger seat, waiting.

I hope she likes it.

I hope Paige likes what I chose for her. I also hope Emily's happy I did it. This seemed like a simple enough thing to do when I made the plan in my mind. I don't know why it feels more complicated now.

Emily and Paige are waiting in the living room when I get back. Emily sits on the couch, looking like a mom on Christmas morning, only dressed for a plane ride.

"Uncle Mateo!" Paige runs across the room and hugs me around the waist. It's a good day, then. I've sat through a couple of silent trips to the ice cream store with her when things were rough. "Mom says you're going on a trip."

"You're going on a trip, too. Did she tell you where we're going?"

"We're all going?"

"All three of us," I say. "The clue is in this bag."

Paige takes it in small hands and glances over

her shoulder at Emily, who nods at her. Paige opens the handles and reaches inside. Christ. My heart is racing faster than it does when they announce who's up for the Oscars. I'm never nominated, but I still hope.

She comes up with the headband first. "A Mickey headband?"

"Minnie." I turn it around so she can see the bow. Her eyes get wide. The longest second of my life passes, and then Paige pushes it onto her head and peers back into the bag. She pulls the plush Mickey out slowly. Is this what terror feels like? Is she too old for these things? Can't be, right?

It's finally all the way out of the bag. Paige finishes her big reveal and thrusts it in Emily's direction.

"Mom," she breathes. "Look. I'm keeping this in my room."

"I thought you might want to take it to Disneyland first," I say.

"Disney?" Paige shrieks.

"Yes," Emily and I say at the same time. She laughs, sounding as relieved as I feel. "We're going to take a long plane ride first."

"Will we sleep on the plane?" asks Paige, staring at the Mickey plush.

"Yeah, and when we wake up, we're going to

Disneyland," Emily says. The vacation was meant to be the main part of the gift, but my chest warms at getting to watch her deliver this news. Easy news. Good news. It's been in short supply the last few years.

"Can we leave right now?" Paige says.

"What do you think, Mateo?" Emily asks me. "Are you ready to take us to the plane?"

"I was born ready. My car's outside."

Paige runs out ahead of us. Emily grabs the handle of her rolling suitcase. Her cheeks are pink with excitement. I wish I had a picture of it. Instead I focus on memorizing that pink all the way to the airfield.

"That's our plane," I say as we pull up next to it.

"A plane just for us?" Paige has her nose pressed to the car window. She's still wearing the Minnie ears. This is the best thing about flying private, bar none. Driving up on the tarmac and soaring off into the sky. With Emily and Paige, it's a double dream come true. I didn't know I had this dream until it was happening, but here we are.

"Just for us," answers Emily. "Let's see what it's like."

CHAPTER TWELVE

Beau Rochester

"DISNEYLAND PARIS," JANE says with a sigh. She leans back in my arms on the wicker love seat we have on our porch. The sunset is in progress, orange and brilliant. It's my new favorite part of the day. "That's romantic."

"I'll take you to Disneyland Paris."

She laughs. "I'd rather stay here with you. In our house."

Jane likes to talk about our house. I feel another echo of the guilt that dogged me on her college tour. Our house. She should be talking about her dorm room. Her roommate. Not a house with me. I push it aside in favor of the sunset.

"I know they're only going to be gone a couple days, but it'll feel emptier around here."

Jane nods and puts her arms around my neck.

"I'm going to miss her, too. My trip to Houston was the last time we were apart for this long."

It's the first time Paige won't be next door. Jane and I go up to Emily's house, or Paige comes down to ours, every day. I can't think of one time we broke the habit, until now.

"Did Mateo send you a picture of the Minnie ears?" I ask.

"Yeah," Jane says wistfully. "It was the cutest thing. I wish we could have seen Paige in them before they left, but…"

"That would have put a damper on Mateo's romantic Paris trip."

"Oh, I know. Paige would have wanted us to come too." Jane's quiet for a minute. "I probably would have gone, if she asked. It's good, though. For Emily."

I know what she means. It's a tough balance between being in Paige's life and stepping on Emily's toes. So far we've been managing it. But Jane and I are always going to be a symbol of her old life—the one she had while she was on the run.

Emily deserves a trip to Paris without all that hanging over her head.

"I'd have gone, too," I say. "But I wouldn't want to miss this sunset with you."

The ocean waves lap against the shore. A gull takes off into the air, calling as it goes.

"It feels right to me," Jane says. "Being here with you. I'm glad we have a new house. I miss Paige so much, but… what we have here doesn't feel incomplete. Am I making any sense?"

"Yes. I miss the hell out of her. We're not broken, though."

Though I worry about what will happen if Jane really decides not to go to college on campus. I don't want her to resent me for it later. I want her to make the best choice for her, even if things have to be different for a few years.

"She must be so excited," Jane says. "Disneyland. You think Emily's going to like it?"

"She'll be there with Mateo."

"That's what I mean. You think they can go on a vacation together?"

"I think Mateo is an oversized kid who still loves theme parks. They've been spending more time together, anyway. He went over to watch the interview with Emily."

"He should just build a house between our two. Then he wouldn't have to travel so far between properties."

"I think he'd much rather move into the Coach House."

Her eyebrows go up. "Do you think Mateo's interested in Emily?"

"I know he is."

"But he was always so caustic with her."

"He's charming all the time, to everyone. It only stands to reason that the one time he's not, it's because he doesn't know how to handle his feelings."

"Men," she says, shaking her head. She brushes a kiss to my cheek. "The interview was terrible. I'm glad Emily had someone to watch with her."

"Joe's an asshole. The least he could do is stop trying to use her as leverage. It's going to affect Paige, too. I blame him. And the news. Goddamn vultures don't care how it impacts the victims."

"I don't even know what I'd do in that situation." The sun sinks lower, and Jane's thoughtful. "With the interviews and the press. And having a child."

"It makes things more complicated."

"I think..." She lets out a breath. "I think I would like it. Becoming a mother, I mean."

I close my arms around her and hold her closer. "You would?"

"I've always wanted kids. At least one kid," Jane amends. "I didn't think about it in detail, though. I figured it would be something I would do after I graduated and established my career."

My heart beats faster. "Did something change?"

"Yeah. I met you." She smiles at me, her dark eyes warm and loving. "Now, when I think about having a baby, it's your baby. And I think about bringing our baby back to our house. This house. It's not abstract anymore."

"But you still want to wait until after you graduate." I keep my tone neutral, because I don't want her to know how badly I want this. How badly I want to fill her with my seed until she's pregnant. To see her belly grow larger with our baby. To have a family with her.

Jane thinks about it for a minute. "I think… the timing is the least important part. I know I want to have your babies. If that happens before I get a degree, then…" She shrugs. "I would be happy. But… maybe you wouldn't."

"What?"

"Maybe you'd be less happy, I mean. Do you want kids?"

I run my fingers through her hair. She's so goddamn earnest. So hopeful.

Jane Mendoza has always been hopeful, even when I was a grumpy asshole who told her to take care of a kitten or I'd fire her. I'm still a grumpy asshole, but I love her. I love her so much that I want more of her in the world.

"I never did. And then I met you."

The corner of her mouth quirks up. "And now?"

"Now I do." The urge strengthens. Predictably, it makes my dick hard. "Right now, actually."

Her eyes widen. "You want me to be pregnant right now?"

Yes. I do. As soon as the words cross her lips, I can see it. Jane, resting her hands on top of her belly. Me, feeling a baby kick, my palm against bare skin.

"Yes," I admit. "But I don't want to push you. It's an asshole thing for me to want."

"Why?"

"Because you're young. You're deciding on college. You've got all that ahead of you. It's not right for me to want to get you pregnant right now, on this porch."

"Beau," she scolds, laughing.

"What? Nobody's here. They wouldn't see. But it would disrupt all your college plans. That would make me feel guilty as hell."

Jane traces a fingertip across the collar of my shirt. "You still want it, though."

"Yeah. I still want it."

She climbs into my lap and straddles me. "Are you sure?"

I put my hands on her hips. "I'm damn sure."

The layers of clothing between us feel thin enough to fuck her through. It's not true. I'm wearing jeans. Jane settles herself against me. I can feel her heat through the cloth.

"It would be hot to have sex out here," she says. "We could do it like this."

"But then you wouldn't be able to see the sunset." I pick her up and put her on her feet, then guide her hands to the porch railing. "If we did it like this, we could both watch."

"I don't care about the sunset anymore." She wriggles her hips into me, and I don't care about the sunset anymore, either.

"We can see it from the bedroom."

I pull Jane's shirt over her head before we even reach the stairs. We live together, and it does nothing to slake my thirst for her. I want her all the time. And this idea of having a baby together—of her, having my baby—has made me harder than I think I've ever been.

That night when I take her, I fuck her long and hard. I want a baby to take root in her body. I want to bind her to me in the most elemental way. And when she comes, she shudders in my arms. She cries out my name before falling into a sudden sleep. I wake her again and again over the night. She moans, half in dreams, when I push my cock into her. She's probably sore, so I become more gentle—but just as insistent. I move her body where I need her, and she lets me. She lets me. She's pliant in my hands, and I thrill over the power, even as guilt eats at me.

CHAPTER THIRTEEN

Jane Mendoza

W HEN WE MADE our first campus visit, the advisor, Mary, gave me an invite to a small meetup. It's for people who are thinking about attending college here—prospective first-year students and transfer students, people like that. People like me. I wasn't sure if I should bother going. What did it matter, if I was only going to attend class online?

But Beau seems serious about getting a feel for the college experience. So two guys from the security team drive me to campus and let me out in front of the café.

The small building looks out onto a street that divides campus from college town. According to the sign, they serve fancy coffee in the morning and microbrews in the evening.

I wipe my hands on my jeans and peek in

through the front windows. Maybe this was a mistake. What am I supposed to say to all these people while we drink trendy microbrews? That I'm only here because I took a job as a nanny and fell in love with my boss? That I'll probably never see these people again, unless it's on Zoom for class?

A girl pushes open the front door of the café and pokes her head out. "Are you here for the meetup? I'm calling us the Microbrew crew, by the way. Just made it up."

No, I want to say. A newspaper vending machine on the sidewalk holds copies of the New York Times and the university paper. *I just stopped to look at the newspapers.* "Yes," I say instead, forcing a bright smile. "Am I in the right place?"

"Yes!" Her purple hair is on top of her head in a messy bun, and that shade of purple perfectly matches her wide grin. "I thought I would come out here and make sure nobody got stranded. I was doing the same thing fifteen minutes ago. My name's Grace. What's yours?"

"Jane Mendoza."

We shake hands, and she laughs at the formality. "We're outside. Is that cool with you?"

"Totally cool," I say, and follow her through the café to the patio in the back.

The patio is fenced in with wooden slats that fail to keep the foliage around them at bay. Plants reach through the gaps in the fence. Fairy lights are wrapped around poles running overhead, like a semi-open roof. Grace leads the way to a group of three wrought-iron tables pushed together to form a weird, bumpy shape.

"Everybody, this is Jane," Grace announces. "Jane, this is everybody." She rattles off the names of all seven people at the table. "Sit here, by me." I take the seat next to an empty chair, and Grace sits back down.

"I'm sorry," I say to the guy I'm sitting next to. "I don't remember your name. It happened fast."

"Kevin," he says. He's handsome, with blue eyes and dark hair. "Welcome. What's your major going to be? If you choose this school, anyway."

It almost sounds like he might be joking. Like all the people at this table are sure they're going to be accepted, and they're even more sure they'll attend.

"I'm going into social work. If I get in, and if I accept."

"Really? I've heard that's a great program. They run some really good on-campus services. If I wasn't already committed to pre-med, I might have done that instead."

"Stop him," says Grace. "If you don't stop him, he'll tell you about his hopes and dreams for medical school literally all night. He already has his acceptance letter. He just hasn't officially accepted. *Someone* applied to twelve million places."

"I like talking about hopes and dreams," I say, which is maybe the wrong thing. I want to fit in. I'm not sure I do fit in, though.

A guy on the other end of the table brings up intramural sports. "Indoor soccer is going to be killer," he says. "Who's signing up if they're accepted? Grace? Jane?" Grace shakes her head. I expect for him to pass me by, but he focuses in. "What about you, Jane?"

"Oh, I'm not a… sports person. I wouldn't be any good." I wouldn't be here to play soccer, even if I had played in school.

"Doesn't matter." The guy whose name I can't remember grins. "They have team practices. Not everybody went to soccer camp, and you're only as strong as your weakest player."

"That would probably be me," I say.

"No way," he protests. "You could get better with a little practice."

Grace pats my arm. "You do *not* have to play

soccer. Social work, huh?"

"It's been a goal of mine for a long time," I tell her. Is it cool to admit this? I have no idea. "I want to help kids in the foster system. I'm not sure exactly what that'll look like, though. Working for the state or another agency."

"That's amazing," says Grace. "You and Kevin both want to change the world."

"What about you? Do you have any world-changing plans?"

"I'm going to be in Fine Arts," she says. "Theater, with a minor in film. I like weird, experimental stuff that's never going to make me any money. Honestly, I should get a job at this café so I can save my extra cash." Grace is jovial about this. It's a shift. Growing up, I wanted to go to college because I thought it would make my life better. I can't imagine signing up for a four-year degree thinking that I'd just work at a café forever, but then… that happens, doesn't it?

Or maybe this is a different situation entirely for Grace. Her parents might be paying for college, so the fact that her art isn't commercial isn't a big deal.

Beau's paying for your college, that small voice whispers.

"What made you want to go into experimental theater?" I ask, because I'm definitely not going to ask her if she has student loans.

"Love," she says simply. "I just love crazy shit like that. My parents made me promise to get a minor in something I could use to have a career, so I'm going to do film. I might just switch my focus. You know? Apply for jobs in the film industry and do theater work on the side. The café can be my fallback plan."

So many plans.

"You make me feel like such a simple, boring person," Kevin says. "All I have is one goal."

"Oh, come on. You have all those interlocking goals," Grace teases. "Jane, Kevin already told me about his three-tiered goal system."

"First—top ten percent in all my classes next year, pending my decision." Kevin starts ticking them off on his fingers. "Second, early matching for med school. Third—"

"It's *tiered*," says Grace. "Building blocks to success. I could make an experimental play about it. Wait. Have you ordered a beer yet? No, you haven't." Grace summons a waiter. "Bring Jane your finest microbrew," she says. "And another one for me, too."

The waiter returns a minute later, and I sip at the microbrew and listen to the others talk.

Maybe I'm not so different from them. They're all excited to be here, too, but in a wry way. *If we get in. If we accept.* None of them are worried about being rejected. They're enthusiastic about the plans they have for the future. The more of my microbrew I drink—what is a microbrew, anyway? It's better than the beer I had with Beau—the more I feel a warm nostalgia for the kind of campus life they're describing. It sounds fun. It sounds almost like an escape from the real world. Living on a campus like this would be like living in a dream. Nothing to do but take classes and get an internship in the field of your choice?

Dreamland. Heaven.

Grace keeps asking questions about my plans, and before I know it, I've been talking to her for half an hour. The conversation around the table turns from majors to the citywide book club that's going on in the fall. Everyone on campus and in the city who wants to is going to read the same novel. Then there are all kinds of events to discuss it.

"Should we go as a group? If we're all here, I mean." Kevin asks. "We probably couldn't bring beer to the discussions."

"The author's going to visit," one of the other women says. "She's going to give a talk. We could meet here afterward."

"Sold," says the sports guy. It makes me laugh because it's months away, and we're prospective students, and this group is already deciding to spend the time together.

I could be part of this.

If I wanted, Beau would move here with me. Knowing Beau, he'd probably buy a house rather than rent. We'd own a college-town house as close as humanly possible to campus so that I didn't have to struggle to get to classes.

But it wouldn't be just like this, would it? Because Beau would be there. Or he wouldn't be there, because… why would Beau Rochester want to sit at a thing called a Microbrew Meetup? And if he were close, but not with me, I'd miss him the entire time. Just like I do now, only I'd have the option to walk from the café into his arms in less than ten minutes. The way I feel about Beau makes it hard to leave him and even harder to be apart for any length of time.

Would it really be any different if we moved here? Or would I still feel like an outsider?

Forget all that for now. I lose myself in the flow of conversation. Whatever happens this fall will happen. I'll make a choice, and Beau will support me in that choice, and it will all be okay.

A small part of me insists that not everything will turn out. There's plenty of difficult shit going on right now. Joe Causey's trial. Getting used to life without Paige. There are no guarantees.

"All we have is this moment," one of the guys says. I have no idea how they got there in the conversation, but that's okay.

Someone passes a joint. I hesitate, but then… why not? All we have is this moment.

Whatever was left of my trepidation disappears after that. I find myself agreeing to plans for next week. For the fall, if I get in. I exchange phone numbers with Grace and promise to text her later. Kevin gives me his email. The meetup is only supposed to last an hour, but it goes on longer. Nobody seems like they're in any hurry to leave. Ten more minutes, I keep thinking. Ten more, ten more.

It's been another hour when I turn my phone over to check the time. Beau looks at me from my screensaver. It's a photo of him I took before construction started on our new house. He's standing right where our kitchen is now, his hands in his pockets. His expression is severe, but there's a smile in his dark eyes. It wrenches my heart.

I think of what I told him as I walked out the

door. It lasts until midnight, but I don't think I'll stay long. Except now it's already eleven, and I'm still here.

It's not late, per se, but I feel guilty. Like my loyalty to him wavered. All it took to make me lose my sense of what mattered was a microbrew and a single drag on a joint. I don't like that I lost my focus.

I get my purse out and put a twenty on the table. "I have to head out," I say. "It was so great to meet you."

"Oh, don't go," Grace says. "It's so early!"

"I have someone waiting for me at home." I bend down to give her a quick hug. "I'll text you soon."

"I'll walk you out," Kevin says, standing up, too.

"Oh, actually—my car is right back there." The parking lot is on the other side of the wooden-slat fence. I had to walk all the way around the building to go in through the front door. "I think I have to go fifteen feet."

"Still. Better not to go alone." Kevin comes with me through a low gate in the wooden fence. He stops when he sees that I'm getting into a vehicle with two muscled security guys. "You get a ride here?"

"Yeah," I say, keeping my voice light. The explanation for the security guards is too long, and too complicated.

"Cool," he says, but it's clear there's a question in his voice. He doesn't sound judgmental, though. "Well, it was great to meet you, Jane. I hope we see you again."

He and Grace could be my friends. It would be so easy to keep meeting up with them. So easy to form our own little group. Who cares if we have different majors?

"I hope so, too. Bye, Kevin."

I wave goodbye to him and climb into the back seat. He paces back to the gate and watches as the car drives through the lot, giving me one last wave before I'm on my way back to Beau.

CHAPTER FOURTEEN

Beau Rochester

I'M NOT PARANOID about Jane going to this meetup or whatever the hell it is. I have a reasonable concern. She didn't think she'd stay very long. I didn't expect her to stay very long, especially not after those pricks approached her at the pub. If any of those people show up to interrupt her group meeting, I'll have them expelled.

But I don't text her.

I don't call her. I don't do any damn thing to ruin this for her.

I want to call her, believe me. I want to call her every five minutes. But the point of all this is for her to make a real decision about how she wants to attend college. Not what she thinks I want her to do, but what she wants to do. This can't be something she does to keep me happy.

Those kinds of decisions never last. People end up resentful and unhappy and I'll be damned if I make Jane unhappy again. Sending her to Houston once was enough.

I make it to ten thirty, and then I call Liam North.

"North," he says, answering on the first ring.

"I wanted to check up on Jane." I try to sound cool and collected and totally unconcerned.

Liam's people have been stationed in the parking lot outside the café all this time. Unless they've started shirking their responsibilities to have a goddamn microbrew. But then—no. They wouldn't. Not these guys.

"She's still at the café," he says, a moment later. "No signs of trouble. She's with a group on the back patio."

"Good. And how are things… around here?" I should have asked about security at our house first. "Emily's house looking okay?"

"Everything's secure on the property," says Liam North. I would say he was laughing at me, but he doesn't actually laugh.

"She's okay, Rochester," he says.

"Of course." I hang up the phone before I can embarrass myself.

I sit down in a chair in the living room and

try to read a book. It doesn't work. Next, I scroll on my phone. It's all bullshit, not worth looking at. The news is running the same tired shit about Emily and Joe. I try the book again. It's not working.

I try not to pace around the house. There are excuses to pace, if I want them. I could look at all the beautiful, modern architecture that makes up the home. I could admire the decorating we've done. I fold a blanket, but there's not much else to fix. With new houses, everything's not broken down already.

I have to move.

It's the only thing that keeps me from giving in to my nerves.

I don't like being away from Jane, and especially not in this circumstance. The paparazzi are already being oppressive and harassing. It's because of these things that we agreed on security dropping her off and picking her up from the café. They're not going to go in with her, but they'll be available by phone.

We agreed, by which I mean that Jane flicked her eyes toward the ceiling and teased me for being overprotective. It took several minutes of negotiation before she would accept being driven. Another five before she would accept them staying in the parking lot.

And the biggest reason I don't love her being so damn far away? Because meeting with a bunch of horny college guys is not where I want my girlfriend to be.

Girlfriend. I don't like that word. It sounds wrong in my head. I want her to be my wife. The mother of my child. I want her locked down in every way there is.

I pace to the front window and look out. No car in the driveway.

Locked down in every way there is sounds right in my head, but it would sound wrong to the world. It would sound obsessive and over the top, the way the security team sounds to Jane. Well, too bad. That's how I feel. Obsessive and over the top. I want our names on paper together. I want it to be official.

I pace to the kitchen and get a beer from the fridge.

What I need to do is relax, goddamn it. Jane is young. She wants to finish college before she settles down and starts a family. That's reasonable. I can't blame her for wanting to get her feet under her before we get swept away by babies and kids and all that comes with it. We both have some sense of how all-consuming it is. Before you know it, months have gone by. Years. Time doesn't slow down when there's a child in your life. There are simultaneously too many hours in the day and not enough months in the year.

I should have gone with her. I drink the beer with a sullen expression that I catch in the window over the kitchen sink. Yes. This is what Jane wanted at her college meetup. A grumpy older man who's impatient as hell to get her home and behind a locked door. Home and in his bed, where she belongs.

I finish the beer and make a point of brushing my teeth for the full two minutes. Anything to pass the time.

Time isn't cooperating.

I find myself back in the living room, then my office, then Jane's study area. The house feels huge without her. It feels soulless. Weeks of planning went into this place, and the moment she steps out the door, it ceases to be a home.

I want her back.

I want her back now.

I sit down with my book again and try to focus on the words. What I need to do is accept how much I have of Jane already. Her heart belongs to me. She wants to be with me so much that she'd rather go to college online and forego the whole on-campus experience.

And she deserves that experience. After everything Jane's been through, she deserves to throw herself into school and the social life that comes along with being in college. Her childhood was difficult enough. There had to be intense pressure to make it out, to make it to college, so she could have any sense of stability. But I don't want her to go to class every day because she's scared of what will become of her if she doesn't get a degree. I want her to go because she loves it.

I stand up and get my keys. If she's not going to be home in the next ten minutes, then I'm going to get her.

I'm at the front door before I get ahold of myself. I am not going to drive to some college town microbrewery to bring her home. She is fine. We are both fine. Both houses up on this cliffside are secure.

I'm being obsessive and over the top.

I throw my keys onto a table by the front door and stalk back into the house. How the hell's a man supposed to live like this? She's been at this meetup for what, two hours, and my heart is going to burst. My hands ache to be around the steering wheel. Even my eyes ache to look at her. It's fucking absurd to feel this way. Even more ridiculous that I want her to be pregnant by the end of the night.

That's the only thought that drags me back from the edge. She doesn't want to get knocked up by some paranoid asshole who comes to bars to take her home because she missed some arbitrary curfew. Hell, she might not want that at all. Not until she has that degree. And I should give her that. I should have some self-control and give her that.

I force myself to read.

It's the greatest exercise of self-control in my whole damn life, to sit here paging through the book. I read a sentence at a time. A paragraph at a time. I cannot stop thinking of Jane. Jane, my wife. Jane, the mother of my child. Jane, pregnant in this living room, her feet up on the arm of the sofa. Jane, pregnant in my bed, sleeping with her back to me and my hand curled around her belly. Jane, Jane, Jane.

The headlights alert me first. They sweep into the house through the many windows. The sound of the heavy SUV tires crunching on gravel comes next. I force myself not to get up. Not to stride outside and pull her out of the vehicle like some deranged person who can't live a few hours without her.

Not to meet her at the door and fuck her in the foyer.

Instead I wait, as if I'm a regular guy who's not obsessed. I hold the book I haven't been reading, my gaze moving line by line over words I don't care about.

Keys in the door.

Buttons on the alarm.

And then she's inside, pushing off her heels and dropping her book bag. She doesn't see me at first. I take advantage of that, watching her in this unguarded moment. Her clothes are relatively casual but they hug her body in a way that's incredibly hot. Other guys got to see her wearing this, which I don't like. Only I get to see her like this, when she's let down her guard.

"You're home," I say, and she jumps.

A little laugh escapes her, effervescent as if she's had something to drink. "I thought you might be asleep. I was trying to be quiet so I wouldn't wake you up."

The bed is impossibly empty without her. The entire house impossibly cold. Doesn't she know she's the goddamn beating heart inside me? "Doing a little light reading."

She comes over to look at my book. "*Advanced Analysis of Financial Markets*. Only you could call that light reading. Is it interesting?"

I set it aside and pull her close. She smells like weed. "You're interesting. Did you share a joint, sweetheart? You have that sweet smoky scent."

A giggle. "Maybe. Are you mad at me?"

I'm not angry, but I'm other things. Possessive. Jealous. Turned on. "No. Yes. You haven't done anything wrong, but I still want to punish that beautiful body of yours."

A shiver runs through her body. "Punish me?"

"Of course," I say in a stern voice. "You're home after curfew. And you did drugs. I think you need to be punished. I think you deserve it. It's the only way you'll learn your lesson."

She goes still. Of course she has no curfew. And she's allowed to smoke a joint if she wants, too. It's a game. A role-play game where I'm the father. She processes the idea, and I hold my breath. It skates a little too close to our age difference, but it also makes my cock hard. Though if she doesn't like it, I'll stop.

I'll still definitely have sex with her. Either way.

We'll only play the game if she wants it.

CHAPTER FIFTEEN

Jane Mendoza

MY BREATH CATCHES in my throat.

If I would have guessed, I'd have thought the sex would get tamer. It would get tamer the more we did it. Now we have our own house together. By some standards, we've settled down. Shouldn't the sex start to get routine?

This isn't routine.

We've never played this particular game before.

I'm not even sure it is a game, at least the way we've played other ones. It feels more stark. More taboo, even as it more closely matches who we actually are. He's older. I'm younger. He's a self-made billionaire. I'm just starting college.

My voice comes out plaintive. "I was only a few minutes late."

"Late enough, young lady."

Maybe it's the drag of weed that I took. Or maybe it's the loosening inhibitions that come from trusting a man fully. Whatever the reason, I curl myself against his side. "Please don't spank me," I say, my voice breathless. "I'll do anything you want."

"Anything?" He raises one eyebrow. "That's quite a promise. You can't even imagine all the ideas I have in my head about what I could make you do."

I'm sure I couldn't imagine them. I'm not sure anyone at the college is doing things like this. I can't imagine the frat boy-esque Brandon role-playing this way.

"I'll be good," I say.

"Show me your tits." The word *tits* comes out crude in the dark room. He used it on purpose. He wants this moment to be slightly dirty. It adds to the authenticity.

It also makes my sex wet. I reach for the hem of my shirt. My hands fist in the fabric. "Are you sure I have to do this? Couldn't I just suck you off?"

His lips quirk. "Is that how you've been getting those A's in school?"

My cheeks heat. It's so wrong, this game. So why does my body feel inflamed? It's like the very fact that it's forbidden makes it hot. "Maybe. The boys on the basketball team like it, too."

"I bet they do. Show me your tits, young lady. Be a good girl for me, and you might get off with a warning. Otherwise I'll spank your ass until you can't sit down."

I make a small sound of denial, refusal, but then I pull up my shirt. My bra comes off with it. The tangle of fabric hits the floor behind me. And then I'm exposed—to the stars and the sea. To Beau Rochester.

"Nice," he says, reaching up to cup the weight of my breast. To rub his thumb across a hardened nipple. He teases me with a casual detachment that makes me burn. "What else are you going to do for me?"

"Isn't this enough?"

He smiles, his teeth white in the darkness. "No, sweetheart. It's never enough."

I start to climb down to the floor, to suck him off. My mouth already waters at the prospect. Maybe it's wrong to enjoy pleasuring him that way. The taste of his salty musk is better than my fingers in a dark room have ever been.

"Not your mouth," he says. "Though maybe later, now that I know you've been practicing. Right now I want that tight little pussy wrapped around my cock. I want you to milk me."

There's a hard clench between my legs. "Are you sure?"

"No condom," he says, which throws me for a second.

It's part of the game, I realize. We don't use a condom. I'm on birth control. We've both been tested. We never use a condom, but he's saying that to make it explicit. To make it clear that we're going to be skin on skin in this illicit fantasy. "But it's not safe."

"Then you should have been home and in bed when your curfew hit. Now pull down your jeans. Let me see the pussy that's going to bring me to heaven tonight."

The air feels electric as I push down my jeans. Nerves make my movements jerky. It's like this is the first time he's seeing me naked. Especially when I stumble out of the denim and into his lap. He gropes me in a hard, possessive way that makes me gasp.

There's a low laugh around us. Him. It's him. He moves my legs to straddle him.

He puts the notch of his cock against my sex. "Down," he murmurs.

"I can't," I moan.

It would be so easy for him to push his hips

up. Or for him to hold my hips down. But he wants me to do it. He wants me to take the final step, so I push down, feeling my tender flesh stretch around his girth. I'm already wet, but it still burns. He's big enough that I have to pause in the middle to catch my breath. And then I slide the rest of the way, my body flush against his.

There's a hard catch in his breath. It's gratifying to know that despite his calm demeanor, he's affected by this. His hands grip my hips so hard there will probably be bruises.

He slaps my ass. "Ride me."

I've always been awkward on top, but in this particular game it makes sense. I move in ungainly strides, forward and back, not quite hitting the right angle, the right rhythm. It takes longer to reach the pinnacle, but he doesn't help me. He just plays with my breasts, leaving my clit to rub against his groin on every downward stroke.

And then he takes mercy on me.

He slides his hand down my stomach to the small thatch of dark curls. He finds my clit with unerring accuracy. One circular stroke. Two. Three.

Climax hits me like a tidal wave, and I choke out my surprise, my denial. He lets out a groan as his own orgasm follows. His cock pulses inside me in a long reward.

We pant in the aftermath.

I rest my head against his chest. "Was that wrong?"

He doesn't have to ask what I mean. The game. The role-play. Pretending that he's my daddy. "Nothing's wrong if it makes you feel good, sweetheart. Did it feel good?"

My body still thrums with the aftershocks of orgasm. "Yes."

He puts a finger beneath my chin and lifts. His dark eyes study mine. "The things that are between us? They're only for us to understand. No one else."

That's the heart of my worry. "I don't want to be a cliché. The girl with daddy issues, because my father died. Because the bastard in my foster home—"

"You're not a cliché. You're a goddamn miracle."

Uncertainty tightens my throat. "But—"

"If you don't want to play that game again, then we won't. Simple as that. But let's get one thing straight. You aren't with me because you have daddy issues. You're with me because you're the only person who sees beneath the billionaire shit and the asshole shit. You're the only one who sees me, and damned if I'm going to let you go."

Tenderness softens my tension. "I do see you. And I love you."

"I'm not so different from my brother. Maybe not even that different from Joe Causey."

"Don't say that. It's not true."

"I'm a selfish bastard. That's why I'm using you. Why I'm playing this game with you. There's darkness inside me."

"Then maybe there's darkness inside me, too. Because I liked the game."

He sighs, pulling me close, cradling me as if I'm fragile. "I'm corrupting you, sweetheart. Day by day. Orgasm by orgasm. Soon you won't even recognize yourself."

CHAPTER SIXTEEN

Emily Rochester

PAIGE SLEEPS IN the Minnie ears Mateo brought her.

The sleeping itself is a tough sell. There's too much to look at on the plane. The first time I try to get her to nap, it's too early. The second time, it's too late. She finally falls asleep underneath a cashmere blanket, the headband still in her blonde curls.

We go directly to Disneyland Paris from the plane. If we'd flown commercial, this would be hell. In Mateo's private jet we were basically in a flying hotel. I feel lighter in Paris, and lighter still when our private tour guide ushers us through a separate entrance. Lisa supplies us with wrist bands that have Mickey's silhouette on them. "These will let you skip any line," she says with a smile. "I'll be with you all day, ensuring that you have a magical experience."

It is magical. It's magical from the first step we take onto Main Street. Lisa accompanies us, along with four people from Beau's security firm. I think this is a little much—five people to make sure the three of us are okay?

But then people notice Mateo.

He's a movie star wherever he goes. The difference in Eben Cape is that he grew up there. Most people at home don't feel any specific urgency about getting his autograph. They don't need his autograph.

Here? Different story. A woman approaches him before we've reached the end of Main Street. She's breathless, holding out a Disney-themed autograph book. "I'm so sorry," she says. "Would you mind? I—would you mind?"

"Of course. What's your name?" says Mateo. He has this down to a science, signing her book and taking a selfie with her in less than thirty seconds.

It happens again as we approach Sleeping Beauty's castle. Paige looks up at it like it's the Eiffel Tower or Notre Dame. I'm glad for Lisa and the guards now. Mateo is just so… approachable.

Two college girls want a photo with him in

front of the castle. He hands their phone off to Lisa, who takes several photos while they're jumping in the air. Paige watches this with her nose wrinkled in confusion. "Why do they all want so many pictures of Uncle Mateo?"

"Because of the movies he makes," I tell her. Because he's incredibly handsome. Because he's incredibly sexy. Because he's a great kisser.

They don't know he's a great kisser, probably.

The college girls go on their way.

"What do you think about teacups, Paige?" Mateo asks as we walk into the cool tunnel that cuts through the castle. "Spinning ones, I mean."

"Spinning teacups?"

"Giant, spinning teacups. You think you might like to ride on one?"

"Yes," says Paige. She walks faster, the sun in her curls, excitement lighting her eyes. We all sit in a blue teacup and Mateo and Paige spin it faster and faster until I honestly might throw up. Paige and I sit together in one row of the Dumbo ride and Mateo sits in front of us, holding up his phone to take a photo of all of us flying through the air. Paige makes us ride It's a Small World twice, back to back, because there are so many figurines to look at. We never wait in a single line.

Guilt nags at me about this, but I don't say a

word. Mateo arranged for this whole day to be as easy as possible. As stress-free as possible. And it's not just less stressful to be whisked to the front of the line. It feels much safer. Two of the security team go with us on every ride, but standing in line is an invitation to be available to people. I'm not hiding anymore. That doesn't mean I want Paige photographed every second we're here. Close proximity to Mateo means enough people are taking pictures of him already without waiting in the longer lines.

"There's someplace I want you to see," Mateo tells Paige after we've gone on all the rides in Fantasyland. "Are you hungry?"

She is hungry, and so am I. One of the security guards has gone ahead and cleared a space for us at the restaurant based on the Ratatouille movie. Paige is beside herself at the décor.

"Look at the chairs, Mom. Look at the chairs!" The chairs look like they're made from life-size bottle caps. Larger-than-life cocktail umbrellas spout over the tables. We sit in a booth that has enormous plates stacked between ours and the next one. They must be ten feet tall. Paige turns around in her seat to tap it with her knuckles. "I didn't know they made plates this big," she says solemnly.

Mateo sits next to her and reads the entire menu off in French. Paige laughs the entire time. "So?" he asks when he's finished. "What do you want to eat?"

"You forgot to read it in English."

His eyes go wide. "My God. I did. Here. I'll read it again."

Paige can read, but she lets him do it anyway. I think she likes the sound of his voice.

I like it, too.

Mateo spends the meal drawing on a coloring page with Paige. About halfway through, I realize they're not actually drawing. They're listing the rides in order of greatness.

"After this," Mateo declares, "we're going on the greatest ride."

"The greatest ride?" Paige echoes.

"My favorite," he says.

We walk off our lunch for twenty minutes, and then Lisa pops us to the front of the line at Big Thunder Mountain. Paige clutches my hand as she watches the mine cars on their track. I can tell she's nervous. But then she sets her jaw. "I'm doing this," she whispers.

That's my girl.

The three of us squeeze into the very first row of the train, and we're off. I know we're in

Disneyland. I know this isn't very intense, as far as roller coasters go. It feels amazing. Paige shrieks with joy and terror without letting up.

Mateo slings his arm around both of us and holds on tight.

"Again," Paige gasps when the mine train comes to a stop. "One more time."

We go twice more, and then Mateo requests that she take a walk with him. "To save your voice," he says.

Paige agrees. We walk to the Finding Nemo ride, which involves zero shrieking, and after, we keep walking. Mateo gives out a few more autographs. My feet hurt. It's wonderful.

At some point he turns, and we're walking through a big Hollywood hall, our security right behind us. Lisa, too. There are lots of people here. The park has gotten busier throughout the day.

"Emily. Emily," someone calls. I don't recognize the voice, but I turn toward it out of habit. "Bold of you to take a vacation after what you did." It's a man I've never seen, moving quickly in the other direction. Mateo nods to the security people. One of them peels off. To do what? Follow him out of the park? I didn't expect to be recognized here. I should have expected it, I suppose.

Mateo puts his arm around me and rubs my shoulder.

"It's not a big deal," I say automatically.

"That guy was a jackass. He's not going to bother us again."

It feels like everyone is watching us now, or I'd burrow into Mateo's arms for as long as it took to make my embarrassment fade away. I settle for stepping a little closer. It feels strange, though. With all these guards, and with Lisa, there's something missing.

Paige.

I turn my head. She's been at my side all day, usually holding my hand. Or holding Mateo's hand. There's plenty to look at in this building. Posters and reproductions of Oscar statues and miniature screens playing movies.

I don't see her.

I stop dead and turn, which messes up the stride of the security guys. "Where is she?" Panic floods my veins. "Where is Paige? She was just here."

She was with us when we walked into this building. I know she was. She looked up and she said something about the ceiling. *Gold on the ceiling, Mom. Look.*

"Shit," Mateo says. "When did you guys see

her last?"

"A minute ago," says the lead guard. "Thirty seconds? She was walking right next to me.

A scream catches in my throat. I want to scream her name, but that's not what you're supposed to do when you lose your child. You're supposed to start announcing what they look like. You're supposed to do it loudly, so that everyone can help you look. But I don't trust these people. I don't want to announce that I've lost my daughter. They'd take pictures. They'd make it worse.

One of the guards turns around and runs. Another one takes off in the opposite direction, deeper into the building.

"Lisa," Mateo says.

"I'm calling now." She's brisk, her phone already at her ear.

"What are they doing?"

"Lisa's calling park security. The others are making sure she doesn't leave the building." Mateo's completely calm. "Paige," he calls. "Where'd you go?"

He takes me by the arm and we walk back to the entrance. We haven't been walking very fast. It's maybe twenty, thirty feet? We start a return trip down the hall. She hides. That's what Paige does. Jane told me about a time she went out into the woods, upset and alone. My vision tunnels. I can't breathe. Where is she?

"Paige." It comes out as a hoarse whisper. "Paige," I call, louder. "Paige."

"Hey, Paige," Mateo says. People are starting to look. I can see them realizing a child is missing. "Blonde, and about this tall," Mateo says to a concerned-looking woman. "Black T-shirt with a Monopoly card on the front. Have you seen her?"

"I'll look," says the woman.

My heart is going to give out. It's just going to die. The building expands in size. It's the size of the entire planet, and I'm never going to find her. What will they say about me, if this gets out? That I couldn't keep track of my child in Disneyland? That I didn't have my eyes on her every second? I only looked away for a *second*. That man called my name.

I look in every alcove we pass. It feels like there are thousands. Screaming would only scare her, but if I don't find her, if someone has taken her, I'm never going to stop.

"Paige," Mateo says, and his voice sounds different. Like he's addressing her directly.

"Where?" I wheeze. He's facing away from me. I don't see her. I don't see her.

And then I do. Her shoes, down below one of the movie screens.

Mateo leans around behind it. Her shoes turn to the side, and she steps into view a second later. I put my hands on her face, on her shoulders.

"Paige," I begin. "Paige." I can't explain the rush of fear. I can't explain why my hands are shaking. I can't begin to tell her how she can never do this again. Never. Or my heart will explode. Her blue eyes are wide and probably as terrified as mine are.

Mateo kneels down to get on her level and takes her hand. "Paige, when we didn't know where you were, it scared us. It scared your mom. It made her so afraid that it hurts." I don't know how he knew to describe it like that. It's accurate. It hurts like I'm having a heart attack. It hurts like someone has tried to pull my arms off my body. Breathing hurts. "It's really, really important that you stay with us, no matter what."

"I don't want to leave," she whispers. "I want to stay."

"Of course you do," says Mateo. "Nobody ever wants to leave Disneyland. But we can talk about that with you. You don't have to hide."

Paige's chin quivers. She steals a glance at me, and then she rushes into my arms, throwing her arms around my waist. My knees feel wobbly, so I get down on one knee and hug her closer. The security guards have formed a little circle around us.

"I'm sorry, Mommy," Paige says. "I'm sorry I scared you."

"I'm okay now," I promise her, but it's not true. I'm trying to live an honest life. I'm trying not to hide behind lies. "I'm going to be okay."

CHAPTER SEVENTEEN

Mateo Garza

I'VE BEEN TO Paris many times, usually accompanied by a model, or an actress. I've arranged for private tours of everything there is to see in the city. I've spent ridiculous amounts of money on the Avenue des Champs-Élysées.

But I have never, ever been as invested as I am now.

Emily sleeps on my shoulder in the car on the way to the hotel. She rallied after we found Paige. We went on a bunch of rides a second time. But I could see how exhausted she was when we finally approached the gates of the park, the sky already darkening.

Emily's not sleeping on a plane tonight. Not even my luxe private jet, which has seats that fold all the way flat. I want her to have steady ground under her feet.

Or under her bed, I guess.

The weight of her head on my shoulder while the car drives us through the streets of Paris feels far more intimate than kissing her. This is the most vulnerable Emily's ever been with me. Both of them, really. Paige sleeps with her head on Emily's lap.

It happens again. Just like it did in that toy store. I start thinking of them in fantasy terms. In *family* terms. This could be how it is, with the three of us. Heading home from a day out.

Me, keeping watch.

The girls, completely asleep.

Paige hugs an even larger Mickey plush to her chest with the smaller one pinned close to her body. There are three bags of Disney merchandise in the trunk of the car. The last thing I did before we left was have the security team clear out one of the stores on Main Street. With Lisa's help, we had thirty-five minutes of uninterrupted shopping in an empty store.

Emily couldn't deny her daughter anything, and I can't blame her. She came damn close to never seeing her again. What's the cost of a snow globe compared to that?

I wasn't really any better. Even if they decided against purchasing something, I followed along throwing it into a bag. I want to give these two the world, but I'm pretty sure they won't let me. So I'll have to settle for bathrobes and matching dishes.

Emily's shoulders finally relaxed in that store, watching Paige run around and look at all the toys. That was when I knew we weren't going to fly back until the morning.

All these feelings are not what I'd call comfortable.

They're nice to think about. I almost feel drunk with how good they feel to think about. But they're a major departure from the way I've thought about my life for many years now.

I never thought I'd settle down.

I *definitely* never thought I'd settle down with a woman from Eben Cape. Marrying a high school sweetheart was something for the suckers who stayed around. Not for people like me.

Plus, Emily wasn't even my high school sweetheart.

She was Beau's high school sweetheart.

I had a thing for her. Who didn't? She was beautiful and smart and she was going places. I fantasized more than once about being with her. About taking her for a drive in my broke-down mustang. Wind in our hair, never looking back. It was nothing more than a dream. Emily only ever had eyes for Beau. Couldn't blame her. Back then, I had nothing to my name and vague dreams involving either acting or veterinary work. Beau had a brooding stare and an energy about him that made all the girls crazy.

It didn't thrill me that he wanted her so much. I wanted my best friend to go fishing with me and drive our cars around and whatever other small-town entertainment we could find. I didn't want him obsessed with Emily. I gave him shit about it whenever I could. I told him it wasn't going to turn out how he thought. He told me I was dead wrong.

Turns out we were both wrong.

Neither of us could have predicted how the last few years would go.

And now Emily has become Emily Rochester, widow, a woman returned from the dead.

I'm enraptured by her.

Maybe I always have been.

But… no. That was a childhood crush.

This is something else entirely. I'm not sure what to call it, but I know it's the domain of adults. Nothing like the teenage lust I had for her back then.

The driver takes us directly to the front of the

hotel, and I shake Emily awake as gently as I can. "Hey. We're here. Time to wake up."

"What?" She squints out the car window. "This isn't the airport."

"I got us a suite at Le Pavillon de la Reine. It's in the heart of the Marais. Very historic. I thought we could all use a good night's sleep before we get back on the plane."

She's too tired to argue if she even wants to. Emily tilts her head toward Paige and raises her eyebrows. *Can you carry her?*

I nod as if she regularly asks me to carry Paige in from the car while she's sleeping.

Emily shifts Paige so I can take her in my arms. The little girl is so tired she barely stirs when I lift her out of the car and arrange her head on my shoulder. The driver pulls out the bags from the trunk and goes in ahead of us.

We meet him in the center of the lobby. He already has the key to the room. There are times I very much appreciate being rich. And a celebrity. This is one of those times. The hotel staff has already checked me in. I give a thankful nod to the people behind the desk.

"What about our clothes?" Emily says, keeping her voice low. The driver leads us across the lobby to the elevators and presses the call button.

"Upstairs in the suite."

"When did you have time to do all this?"

"It was only a couple of text messages." *When you were sleeping on my shoulder*, I want to tell her. *I texted them with one hand. It took goddamn forever to type that way, but I didn't want to have to push you away. It felt too good to hold you.*

"Thank you," Emily says as the elevator rises. "It's been a long day."

For her, it's been more than a long day. It's been a series of long months.

And all this—the trip to Paris, the fancy hotel—it's not because I want Emily Rochester to be with me. It's not because I've fallen in love with her or something ridiculous like that. It's because she deserves good things to happen to her.

Good things like a nice hotel. Like a few minutes in a Disney store without anyone watching her. A few hours to have fun without worrying about something.

My driver waves the key card over the lock and the door clicks open. We step into a generously sized living area. It's not huge by American standards, but it's a good size for the middle of Paris. They've taken special care with the antique furniture. It might be smaller than some of the gargantuan presidential suites I've stayed in, but it's beautiful.

"There are two bedrooms." I put my hand on Paige's back to keep her in place while I talk to Emily. I make sure my voice is casual. I want her to know I don't expect anything from her, despite the fact that we're in a hotel together.

"I'll sleep with Paige," Emily says, her tone cautious.

"Which one do you want?"

She points to one. I hold Paige while Emily opens her rolling suitcase and takes out a pair of pjs. Paige barely wakes up while Emily whisks her out of her clothes and into the pajamas. Then Emily takes her daughter in her arms and tucks her under the covers.

"You need anything?" I ask her, my voice low.

"No," she says with a small, sad smile. "You've done more than enough, Mateo. This place is gorgeous. This entire trip has been a dream."

"Sleep well," I tell her, instead of saying the crazy shit that's in my head. Words like *stay* and *love* and *fuck*. I gave her something without any expectation on her part. The fact that I want more from her… well, that's my problem.

"You too."

I turn around and go before she gets the impression I'm going to hit on her after today. I've been there for her in recent days. We've kissed. It's the most I've ever wanted to kiss someone. But now? Tonight? I'm going to leave her be.

I'm not even halfway across the living room when quick footsteps come after me. Emily touches me a moment later, her hands sliding around my waist. I turn around and hug her back.

"Mateo," she says.

The longing question is crystal clear in her voice.

I've taken her all over Disneyland Paris today. We haven't kissed once. But now I take her chin in my hand and tip her face up to mine.

I kiss her like nobody is watching. For the first time all day, there are no prying eyes. No assholes to take photos. Nobody to ask me for an autograph. Paige is sleeping peacefully in bed. So I kiss Emily slow and deep, saying all the things with my mouth that I can't say with words, using my body to send messages to hers. What the hell was I thinking, out there in the car? That I don't want her? I don't want a life with her?

I was full of shit.

She tastes so damn good. She tastes like home.

"Yes," she whispers against my lips. "That's what I wanted."

"Is that all?" I murmur back, my lips brushing

hers as I speak.

Emily takes a breath. "Do you think I could lay in your bed?"

"You want me to take the couch?"

"No." A quiet laugh. "With you."

"Yeah," I say, my voice thick with desire. "I think you could do that."

We go into the second bedroom. I flip back the covers. Emily strips off her T-shirt. She's got a close-fitting tank top on underneath that's tight around her breasts. Her shorts go next. And then, in a pink pair of panties and her tank top, she slides between the covers.

I get in next to her. Neither of us reaches for the lamps on the side of the bed, and I don't want to. I want to lay here in the dark with her.

I also want to fuck her.

But I'm not taking this faster than she wants.

Emily scooches back against me. I fold one arm over her.

There's a silence, and during that silence, Emily relaxes. It takes her some time. She's not in the habit of letting go when she lays down to sleep at night. I hate that for her. When I realize what's happening, I put a hand on her shoulder and start massaging it.

She sighs. It's a happy sigh. "Paige had a great

time today," she says as I knead at a knot in her muscle. I want her to relax, if only for a single day. For a single night.

"I had a great time, too," I tell her. "What about you?"

"It was mostly great." Another pause. "I wish I'd kept it together when Paige was hiding."

"You did keep it together."

"No, I didn't. I was losing it. I couldn't even think straight to do the things you're supposed to do when your kid goes missing." Her laugh is sad. "You did all that."

"Did I?"

"Yeah. You're supposed to tell people what your child was wearing and what they look like and how old they are. I couldn't even remember. It was just... pure panic."

I don't know what to say. I don't want to dismiss her feelings, but I don't think anyone can expect to stay level-headed when their child is missing.

Especially a person who's been through everything Emily has.

We came to Paris for an escape, but danger followed her. It had to feel like hell.

"I just keep thinking..." Emily takes a long, slow breath. "What would I have done if you weren't there?" I run my hand down her back, over her waist. The curve of her body feels familiar, somehow, and completely new. "Honestly, Mateo…"

She trails off. I wait for a minute for her to finish, then two.

"Honestly what?"

"Honestly…" Emily yawns. "Honestly, I don't know if it would have turned out okay. If you hadn't been there. It's like I needed you, which is scary. But I'm glad you were there."

"I'm glad I was there, too."

There's more I could say.

I would, given the chance, talk to Emily Rochester for several hours.

We're in Paris tonight, in the dark, far from the things that are happening in Eben Cape. Maybe it's the perfect opportunity to talk to her. People can be more open when they travel. I sure as hell feel different. I spent the car ride imagining what it would be like if we were a family.

"I've been thinking about staying in Eben Cape," I say.

I haven't actually been considering it. Not long-term, anyway. But now that I've said it, the idea flourishes in my mind. I could still work as an actor out of Eben Cape. Not everyone has to live in LA. There are such things as private jets and cell phones. It would mean becoming what I swore I'd never be—one of those people who comes home after high school and never leaves.

But so what? Beau is in Eben Cape. And Jane. Emily and Paige. The people that I care about are in Maine. I should be there, too. "What do you think about that?"

Emily doesn't say anything.

She's fallen asleep.

CHAPTER EIGHTEEN

Jane Mendoza

O UR HOUSES SHARE the cliffside, as well as the single road that winds down. At the bottom of our mountain there are two mailboxes. A traditional ornate mailbox belongs to the Coach House. And the more modern mailbox with a metal frame and a herringbone door is ours.

I always dreamed of having my own house. Someday.

But I never anticipated the satisfaction I'd get from seeing mail arrive. Not a small metal box in an apartment complex. Not to someone else's house where I'm the nanny.

Mail coming to my house.

I walk down the steep road in my flip-flops. Maine weather is strange. I've grown so accustomed to the cold, rainy days. Summer heats the cliffside to temperatures that rival Houston.

Sweat coats my arms and upper lip by the time I reach the bottom. There's a black SUV waiting in case I need to go anywhere. And a guard standing duty.

He gives me a professional nod. Brian. That's his name. "Ma'am."

"Good morning," I say with a small wave.

Secretly I find it amusing that the security guards all call me *ma'am* when they're twice my age. I never really understood why some women dislike being called that. Because it makes them feel old? I've wanted to be old for years. Old means having power over your own life. Old means not living in foster homes, at the mercy of abusive men. It's a relief to be old enough to be called ma'am.

I will just ignore the fact that he also calls Paige *ma'am*.

Technically I could have called and had him bring the mail. It's part of their protection services. They'll even pick up groceries and things from the drugstore. Keeping me indoors is part of the safety plan. Unfortunately it's also stifling. So I take my daily walk to breathe fresh air.

And as a bonus, I get to check for mail from colleges.

I've heard back from half the schools so far.

Mostly acceptances. A few rejections.

No word from Mainland College.

And that's where I want to go, I've already decided.

The admissions advisor Mary Monroe had acted like I was a shoo-in, but I know better. My grades were decent, but I didn't have a fancy SAT prep class. Or the money to do extracurriculars.

My application isn't as strong as other students'.

The fact that Kevin already has his acceptance makes me nervous. Though he's in a completely different department than me. I pull the black metal handle, revealing a neat stack of mail. Because the house is new, and the address is new, we don't get a lot of junk.

There are a couple letters for Beau.

A promotional postcard inviting me to a campus tour in upstate New York.

And a letter from Mainland College. The logo of an abstract mountain range looks unassuming. Ordinary. I imagine some clerk stuffing envelopes and stamping them, her mind on other things. Music playing on her phone. Calm and relaxed, nothing like the panic I feel now.

Should I wait until Beau gets back? He's out with Mateo.

No, I definitely can't wait that long. I'm not even sure how much longer he'll be gone, but even one more second is too long to wait. I don't even bother climbing the mountain again. I work my finger beneath the envelope flap, standing on the patch of grass beside the mailbox.

Besides, I reason, if I *don't* get in, I'll be able to hide my disappointment from Beau.

Though, maybe not. It feels like my disappointment would be miles wide. This is the best school, the one I'm most excited to attend, the one where I already have friends.

And the one that's closest to Paige.

I open the folded piece of paper with shaking hands.

Dear Jane,

Your thoughtful application and remarkable background are the hallmarks of a great student.

My heart pounds out of my chest. I don't ever want a letter to start with a compliment. That means there's a *but* coming. Something like: *but we have even better students than you.*

I force myself to keep reading.

Your unique perspective would be a

great addition to our student body. Therefore it is with great pleasure that I offer you admission to Mainland College, Department of Social Work.

A shout of joy escapes me, and Brian jerks to attention, looking alert and wary.

I wave the paper in his direction. "Good news. I got accepted."

His expression doesn't change, but I sense the smile in his eyes. "Congratulations."

Grown-ups who get called *ma'am* should probably handle such news with grace.

Instead I find myself doing a little dance in the sunlight, unable to contain the excitement. It's coursing through my body like electricity, and I laugh with abandon.

The corner of Brian's mouth turns up.

Then he looks away from me, and his expression turns grim.

I follow his gaze to where a car pulls onto the drive. It's an old sedan I don't recognize. It pulls to a stop a few yards away from us. A woman steps out. At first I only get the impression of a slender body in a suit. It covers her almost completely, the pencil skirt reaching down to her knees, a white collared shirt buttoned to the top. Despite the coverage, or maybe because of it, it's undeniably sexy.

The heels would make me fall over, but she navigates them across gravel like a pro.

Only when she's a few feet away do I recognize her. Lauren Michaels, the prosecuting attorney in Joe Causey's case. I sat in her office once, while Beau had a meltdown and ultimately declared his love for me over corkboard furniture and tepid instant coffee.

"Ms. Mendoza," she says with a professional smile.

She reaches out a hand, and I start to shake it. Then Brian steps between us. "I'll need to see some identification, ma'am. What's the nature of your visit?"

From the way her blue eyes flare, she's definitely one of those women who does not appreciate being called ma'am. She looks Brian up and down in a leisurely way, and he stiffens. "Who the hell are you?"

"It's okay," I say from behind Brian. "I know her."

He ignores me. "Private security. Identification?"

With a sigh of exasperation, she turns around and reaches into her car. Which means she's bending over with her behind in a tight skirt. I'm one-hundred percent straight, and even I can notice it's a great ass. Judging by the way Brian's jaw works, he's noticing, too.

Lauren whips around, holding up a card attached to a lanyard. I'm assuming it confirms her position in the District Attorney's Office.

Brian studies it with a concentration that borders on insulting, as if she perhaps had it forged. "Lauren Montgomery Michaels, first assistant district attorney."

With seeming reluctance, Brian hands the lanyard back. "Montgomery?"

"They wanted a boy," she snaps.

He's definitely hiding a smile in his dark eyes when he steps aside so she can talk to me. Lauren raises her eyebrows. "I can see Beau Rochester is doing a good job of protecting you."

I shrug, feeling shy about it. The whole security thing is strange. Most of the time it feels like overkill. But then other times, the constant presence of the guards is a reminder that I'm not entirely safe, either. "Are you looking for him? He's out."

"Actually, I came to see you."

My eyebrows go up. "You have my statements."

"Yes, but statements are just words on paper.

We need you to testify."

Panic tightens my throat. "You said we wouldn't have to do that. We talked about this. You told Beau that you wouldn't put me on the witness stand."

"That was before."

"Before what?"

She sighs, but it's a different sound than the one she made for Brian. That one had been full of feminine attitude. This one's a soul-deep weariness. "The interview Causey did is having an impact."

My skin feels prickly. "People are believing him?"

"Yes, but that's not really the problem. The court of public opinion isn't supposed to matter when the jurors are sequestered. But someone leaked the video to them. I'll give you one guess as to who, but we can't prove it. And it's swaying them. I know juries, and this one's sympathetic."

"But even if what he said is true, that his father was abusive, that doesn't make it okay for him to be a dirty cop, for him to steal and launder money and kill Rhys Rochester."

"I know that. And you know that. But a very expensive defense attorney is doing his best to convince the jury otherwise. There's a reason he owns a yacht, for God's sake."

I run a hand over my face. The joy from the admissions letter hasn't gone away. It's still there, mixing with my nerves about Causey's trial, creating an unstable chemistry inside me. I feel like throwing up. "How is me testifying going to help anything?"

"I'm going to use you to establish a pattern of corruption and violence. Causey claims he killed Rhys to protect his sister. Claims that she got afraid when she saw it happen, but that he never would have actually hurt her. If we can show that he continued to be corrupt after that, then it will help the jury see him for what he is."

"Beau's not going to like it."

She gives me a small smile. "I think if anyone can manage him, you can."

"I'm not sure I like it, either."

Her smile disappears. "It won't be easy. His defense attorney will tear into you. I'll have to prepare you to be on the stand, do some practice sessions. Causey will stare you down."

I look down at the acceptance letter. It's crumpled a little bit in my fist, but that's okay. It will still work. I'll still go to Mainland College and become a social worker.

Except how can I really stand up for the

community if I can't testify against Causey?

This is the terrifying work. It's also the crucial work.

Social work is not only about smiling at children and wishing them the best. It's facing down abusive parents. It's standing up to the courts. It's fighting for what's right. That doesn't just start when I graduate. Apparently, it starts right now.

CHAPTER NINETEEN

Jane Mendoza

B EAU ALREADY KNOWS that Lauren Michaels was here. The security guards probably called and told him about the visitor.

Sometime after her visit, it starts to rain. It sends a chill through the warm summer air, making it feel like winter again. I'm sitting on the screened front porch in a cushioned wicker chair when the dark green Jeep careens up the mountain. Beau pulls to a stop. I can only see his shadow through the windshield, but I feel his intensity as he steps out and slams the door. Determination has darkened his expression, making him appear angry. A shiver runs through me. It's fear. I'm not afraid of Beau. He wouldn't hurt me, but I can't help the instinctive response. I lived too long under the rule of violent men in foster homes to be comfortable.

"Absolutely fucking not," he says again, standing on the step. He's still getting rained on, two feet away from the overhang, but he doesn't seem to notice. Rain hits his face. Wind whips his hair. An unzipped jacket does nothing to protect him from the elements. He looks stronger than them, anyway. More powerful than the storm.

I try to keep my breathing even. I don't want to show him that I'm afraid. Men don't understand. Maybe even women wouldn't understand if they've never been hit by a man. That is something Emily and I have in common. "You don't even know what she said to me."

"I can guess. Why the hell else would she show up when I'm gone?"

"You're being paranoid. She doesn't know your schedule."

He snorts. "Don't underestimate her. She's using you."

"She's using me to put away a murderer, Beau. How is that wrong?"

"It's wrong because his focus is off you now. He's busy with the goddamn trial. Busy covering his ass. Busy talking to reporters. He's not thinking about you anymore, but he will. If you're on that stand, all his rage will focus on you—again. He's dangerous, Jane."

"I know he's dangerous, which is why it makes even more sense that I help put him away."

"This isn't your fight. It's about Joe Causey being a dirty fucking cop and a murderer. What he did to you shouldn't even have to factor in. That's what Lauren said, remember? That you wouldn't have to testify, because they have a strong enough case without it."

"It's the interview. It's swaying public opinion. And the opinion of the jurors. She thinks they might lose."

"The jury that's supposed to be sequestered?"

I throw up my hands. "They're staying at the Oceanside Motel. It's a small town, Eben Cape. Everyone knows what's happening. A single cop car in the parking lot doesn't hide it. Reggie's Pizza delivers every night. Next Day Dry Cleaning drops off every morning. There are ways to reach them."

He swears, long and creatively. "They wouldn't even need to use the pizza place or the dry cleaning. The cops are Joe's buddies. They probably handed out DVDs of the interview."

"All the more reason I should testify."

"You're not testifying," he says, finality ringing in his voice. "That's final." Rain plasters his hair to his forehead. He's gotten drenched in the time that he's been standing there. I want him to come inside, but in this moment he feels unapproachable. Alien.

He doesn't seem like the man who held me so tenderly last night. As if he realizes this, he suddenly strides away from me. He rounds the house, and I'm left abruptly alone.

For a moment I listen to the rain pound on the rooftop.

It's a metal roof, so it's louder. More expensive, too. I thought metal roofs were for double-wide trailers. Apparently they're also for ultra-luxury new houses, complete with solar paneling and water containment systems.

Those water containment systems will be filling up now, saving the water until it can sprinkle it back out over the lawn. There's something beautiful about that, I think.

This dark, gloomy weather will make it beautiful. Someday.

✧　✧　✧

Beau Rochester

RAGE RUNS THROUGH my veins.

And underneath that, darker and more potent, is fear.

I don't want Jane to be in the same room with

Joe Causey, not ever again. I don't want her to be under his scrutiny, to be forced to face him, to be the object of his animosity once again. It might seem like overkill, this protective instinct inside me, especially with advanced security systems and guards roaming around. But I understand what he's capable of. He killed my brother. My brother was not a good man. He deserved what he got, but that doesn't make Causey any less dangerous.

Water stretches out in front of me. It's endless. I know this horizon as intimately as I know Jane's face. I've looked at it during night and day. I've explored its terrain, but it still contains mysteries. The cool rain is a welcome relief from the heat earlier. I'm a northerner through and through. I prefer the cold.

Wind whips around me, howling in my ears—loud, but not so loud that I can't hear Jane approach across the gravel.

I'm standing too close to the edge. That's fine for me, but I don't want her to slip. One wrong footing and a large gust of wind could send her flying over the edge. And I would… not survive that. It's hard to admit for someone who's been closed off. Who's been determined not to care about someone. Paige put a crack in the emotional wall. Jane broke the rest of it to pieces. I can't let anything happen to her. But I also can't stand to see the wariness in her eyes. The way she looked at me from the porch...

It made me feel like a monster. As if there's only a thin veneer keeping me from becoming Joe Causey.

I don't do unethical shit. It's always struck me as the coward's way out. Why cheat when you can win the right way? But knowing Jane has changed me. If I had to protect her, I would lie, cheat, or steal. I would kill for her. And it's absolutely terrifying.

She stands amid the downpour with her chin held high. A goddess, this woman. She humbles me with her bravery. She could have gone inside, *should* have gone inside. To stay warm and away from the ogre who's making demands on her. Instead she's facing me. Delicate? Yes, but also unbelievably strong.

"I was already responsible for one woman's death. We believed that Emily died. And she *could* have died. It was my fault. It would have been my fault, and I had to live with that. I can't add another life to my tally. I can't watch anything happen to you."

"I'm not going to die. And Emily didn't die. You aren't responsible for us."

"I am, Jane."

She looks away, and when she faces me again, her expression is resolute. "You've given me so much already. The ability to go to college. The house. And… you. Your love. The way you care for me. It's more than I deserve."

I had expected her to argue, but she isn't doing that. At least, not in a way that I can combat. This vulnerability is breaking my heart. "Jane."

"But I can't take this—this free pass you're offering me."

"A free goddamn pass? It's a murder trial. You weren't even in the state when he killed my brother. It's not a free pass if you don't get involved."

"A free pass," she continues, "to look the other way while injustice is done, while people are hurt. While they can continue to be hurt. I've lived too long among those who were hurt. People looked the other way. Good people, I think. Regular, honest people who looked the other way when we came to school with bruises or wore clothes that didn't fit."

"If they saw a child being abused and didn't say something, they weren't good people."

She throws up her hands, catching the rain. It

sparkles against her tan skin. I want to lick it off. Even now, in the middle of an argument, with her sad past pulsing between us, both of us cold and drenched, I want her more than anything. There's something raw about it. As if we're being reduced to our baser selves the more the rain pounds us. As if it's washing away the last layers of societal conditioning, leaving only a man and a woman. "They had their own problems to deal with. I don't judge them."

"I do."

"Maybe they were worried about what would happen if they intervened. Maybe they were worried about retribution, the same way I'm afraid of Joe Causey, but I won't let that stop me from speaking up. I *can't* let that stop me, otherwise surviving the foster home was for nothing."

"For nothing?" I say, my voice thickened with emotion.

Her dark eyes shine with more than rain. There are tears. "I made it out of there so that I could become a social worker and help kids. But how can I do that, how can I face the people who abuse and neglect them, if I can't confront Joe Causey?"

Whatever restraint I have left snaps like a thin,

brittle twig. I grab her in my arms and hold her against me—too tight. I know that, but I can't seem to moderate my grip. I have no control, no finesse. I press my lips against hers. It's not even a kiss. It's a claiming. "Don't ever say that you survived for nothing. You didn't survive to help other people. What you do for them? That's a gift. What you do for me? A goddamn miracle, but it's not your purpose. Not your worth. You're worth more than gold, than diamonds. You're worth everything all on your own."

She's shivering, but I don't know whether it's from the cold or from the intensity of my embrace. "You don't know," she says, her voice shaky. "You don't know what it was like. I go around smiling and laughing and living, but there's a part of me that will always be in that house, that will always be fourteen years old and terrified."

I hold her hard to my body as if I can block the painful memories. But I can't. That's the truth. I can't block the memories. I can't fix her past. I have to live with that helplessness, and it's killing me. How ironic is that? She's the one who has to live with that pain, but I'm the one breaking apart. "You shouldn't have to be terrified. Not ever, not by anything. Especially not Joe Causey. Don't you see? I can't let you testify, Jane. I can't accept that."

She pulls back, and the few inches between us feels like miles. "And I *have* to testify."

We're at an impasse. For the first time in our relationship, a true impasse. It can't be overcome. At least, that's what it feels like. I'm still holding her, one arm around her waist, the other cupping her jaw. I'm touching her, but even as my grip tightens, I can feel her slipping away.

CHAPTER TWENTY

Emily Rochester

Y OU GET A book deal, you have to write the book. That's the whole point of submitting your proposal to agents and editors. Of getting a large sum deposited in my bank account for an advance. Which means there's a book I need to write.

It's more than the book deal. I need to write it for myself, too.

My memoir is a vital thing, like consuming food or drinking water, but for my soul. Or is it my heart? Whatever part of me holds this burning desire to speak my truth about what happened to me. The memories are poison, and I need to let them go if I'm going to keep living.

It's for me. And even for Paige, who deserves a mother less burdened by the past.

And even for other women, who might be in

the same situation. Other women who might think there's no way out, no hope for the future. Every word I write is for them.

That is, when I do manage to write words. Right now? Not so much.

The cursor blinks in the open document. I'm not starting with a blank page. Not exactly. I've already written about ten chapters. The first few words—those were painful.

These are turning out to be painful, too, but for a different reason.

I want to hold on to the high of being in Paris with Mateo.

Except for those few minutes when Paige was missing, it was magical. The joy on my daughter's face while we were on Mateo's favorite roller coaster was a balm. I put her through hell, but that day in Disneyland was a little piece of heaven. Not nearly enough to make up for the time I was gone, but it was something.

A bright memory to outshine the dark ones.

My attention wants to wander to Paris. It doesn't want to focus on the heartbreaking depths of my past. I wish we were in Paris now. Paige would miss being apart from Beau and Jane for so long. She squealed when we came back. They were waiting with a large family dinner for all five of us, and then a sleepover with just the three of them. It's not realistic that we would have stayed in Paris and seen the sights indefinitely. Not realistic that we would have gone back to Disneyland Paris, again and again. Day after day. But it's my dream.

You can do anything in a dream.

And Paris with Mateo was definitely a dream.

Back in Maine, I have the book deal. And I have the truth.

I even have my favorite work area in the house.

The kitchen island is large and spacious. The rebuilt Coach House has larger windows than before. Light pours into the kitchen and makes everything seem more hopeful. I like to sit here and work. I think of the words like ingredients. I put flour and eggs and milk into a bowl before this. All I need to do is stir the correct words together. Pour them out of the air and stir them well. It should be easy enough, in a place like this. I've basically reached the height of convenience by writing in the kitchen while a chocolate cake bakes in the oven.

There's a short supply of flour and eggs and milk. At least, the word versions.

I hope this gets easier eventually. It has to,

right? The more chapters I put down, the stronger I am. If I can get through this, I'll be unstoppable by the end of the memoir. At the very least, I'll be able to say I wrote a book. Most people haven't done that.

I feel another pang of sadness that I have to write this book at all. If I'd had a different father, a different brother, a different husband…

It would be a different book entirely. Well, it wouldn't even exist.

I wouldn't even exist, not the way I am now. I'd be someone else entirely.

I tap out a few words. They look wrong on the page, so I highlight them all and delete them with one keystroke. It turns out there is no magic element to writing a book. There is no montage wherein the plucky writer drinks coffee and sips wine while the camera circles around her, and at the end, there's a printed, bound, glossy book.

Try again. I type out a few words and get to the end of a sentence.

Still not right. The chapters I've written so far have taught me that if the beginning's wrong, the rest won't follow. I have to get that part right.

And so far it's very, very wrong.

How do fiction writers do this? I prop my chin in my hand and stare out the window at the summer green. The difficulty of this project is finding just the right words to describe real events. What would I do if I had to invent the plot first?

I'd make it happier, for one thing.

But my story wasn't happy. It was my story. And I'm not doing it because I think the truth of my life is unique. Actually, I think it's pretty common. I know it's common. The story of my abusive father and, later, my abusive husband is a familiar one among women.

It's a story that gets swept under the rug over and over again.

It'll keep getting shoved out of sight unless we refuse to be silenced.

Bottom line, though—no one will ever hear my story if I don't write it down and publish it in this book. Pressing forward is the only option.

You could ask Mateo to take you back to Paris, a procrastinating voice whispers.

My face heats. The voice has a point. I could ask him, and I don't think he'd refuse. I think he'd have his plane ready in a matter of hours. What's happening between us is extremely strange, but the Paris thing? That was good.

However, I will not be texting Mateo to ask him for a repeat vacation. I will not be abandoning my laptop in my house and flying off to a better destination.

Even if I desperately want to.

"That's hiding, Emily," I say out loud. "And you're done hiding."

I blow a mental kiss to the happy memories of being with Paige in Paris. With Mateo in Paris. The way he was with her, patient and charming. The warmth of him in bed next to me. I'll still have those memories when I'm finished writing.

And I only have until Paige's birthday cake is done to write today.

Her party is tomorrow afternoon, and I wanted to leave plenty of time to frost and decorate. This is going to be the first birthday she'll spend with all of us—me and Beau and Jane and Mateo—and I want it to be perfect for her.

One final glance at the timer on the stove, and I turn my attention to my childhood.

There's no sugarcoating it. Joe and I had a shitty childhood, which Joe is using as an excuse for his behavior. That's one of the many things that makes the memoir, and the court case, so complicated. It was a terrible way to grow up. It doesn't excuse the fact that he murdered Rhys, and he would have murdered me. But it was awful. Worse than I wanted to admit to Mateo, who had a happy family with a bunch of sisters and a large brood of aunts and uncles and cousins. He couldn't possibly understand the solitary life we led.

No one is going to understand. Not unless I stop thinking and write.

My father was not a good boss.

In fact, he was a terrible one. This wasn't a secret in the small town where I lived with my brother. Everyone knew that Jethro Macom was an asshole.

According to local lore, he'd been an asshole since the day he started working at a canning company in Connecticut. He was sixteen at the time and swept the floors between shifts. When he graduated, he moved up to a position on the production line. When I turned fifteen he got fired from his job. It was framed as a layoff, but everyone knew the truth. Everyone heard the rumors. We moved to Maine, where he got a job in Eben Cape.

Plenty of people worked at the factory with only a high school diploma to their names, but not many of them had my father's track record.

The joke was that Jethro couldn't go six months without getting written up. People would place bets on it. Even when he attained a position of power that let him write other people up for workplace infractions, he didn't stop committing his own.

Intimidating other employees. Shouting. Hitting. Sexual harassment.

Over the years, I've come up with many reasons why Eben Cape Canning Co. kept employing my father. The first was the six-month timeline. He always allowed time to pass between his outbursts. The second was the boom-bust nature of operating a factory in a place like Eben Cape. Everyone knows you have to keep the people you have, otherwise you might end up short-handed when it counts. The third is that my father was obviously volatile. Firing him might have caused more problems for the owners of the factory than keeping him on.

For all those reasons, I can understand—though I don't agree with the decision—how my father was able to keep his job.

What I can't understand is why no one thought to ask after his children.

A factory, by definition, is a fairly public place. No one in Eben Cape had any illusions about what kind of man my father was. He shouted in public. He hit people in public. He sexually harassed his employees. Maybe even worse, behind closed doors.

Why didn't anyone worry about what he did at home?

After all, his employees still kept their jobs, if they wanted them. They took home paychecks and put food on the table. It was just that they had to dread each day in the factory.

In a similar way, we always had enough clothes and enough food to eat. It was just that we lived in fear of his temper. We used to look forward to the days he had to work late. It meant he couldn't terrorize us at home. Looking back, I understand that this just meant he was terrorizing other people instead.

He spent his days berating and, in some cases, assaulting his employees. He spent his time with us following much the same pattern. Once, at dinner, I spilled some of my soup on the tablecloth. My father responded by holding my hands to the boiling pot until Joe begged him to stop. Once, my brother Joe failed a test at school. My father responded by whipping his ass with a belt until I begged him to stop.

We protected each other, me and Joe. We tried our best to protect each other. That's not my imagination.

Which is why it's so difficult to square my brother as he is now with the person he was back then.

How did Joe Causey go from being my protective older brother to a murderer? When did the change take place? Was it the night he shot my husband, Rhys, or was it before then? How much should past kindness weigh when balanced against present crimes?

I still don't know the answer to that question. I don't know if I ever will.

All these questions. I sit back in my chair and cover my eyes with my hands. It makes me cry, writing these things. I didn't cry in the courtroom when I testified against Joe. It's when I try to put these two versions of him side-by-side on paper that the tears well up.

I'm not even sure that the question should matter. He murdered Rhys. No amount of childhood heroism will undo that. But like I told Mateo, I still love him.

The timer goes off, interrupting the cascade of feelings.

That *beep beep beep* brings me back into the present moment. The trial is always hanging in the background, but this moment—this one, right now—it's simple.

Time's up. Time to stop excavating the past and putting it on paper.

Time to step away and tend to the life I've built.

I close the laptop like it's about to boil over, shuffle my notes back into their folder, and go to take my daughter's birthday cake out of the oven.

CHAPTER TWENTY-ONE

Mateo Garza

THERE'S ALWAYS SOMETHING to do in LA. Auditions. Interviews. Publicity lunches with pretty, forgettable actresses to generate buzz about upcoming projects. That's been my life since I moved out there. In my profession, the only thing that changes is the scenery. I've had auditions in Italy. Interviews in Switzerland. Publicity lunches in Beijing.

The one thing I couldn't do in any of those places?

Attend my niece's birthday party.

Paige turns eight years old today, and in a twist that's as shocking to me as anyone else, there's nowhere I'd rather be than the patio at Coach House. Emily's decorated with streamers and balloons outside the kitchen. The cake—which is beautiful and painstaking, heartbreakingly simple, lovely—waits inside on the kitchen island. Beau, Jane, Emily, and I gather around the patio table to take too many pictures of Paige opening her gifts. She gets a brand-new Monopoly shirt and hoodie. A zip line that goes outside between the trees. A new set of paint for her rocks. Paige grins at each one like it's everything she ever wanted.

"Wow," Jane says, a mirror grin on her face. "Are you going to set up a rock shop?"

"Sell my rocks?" Paige says. "Never!" She purses her lips and looks back down at the paint. "Well, maybe I would."

"Save up your money and you could buy a real hotel," says Beau. He rubs Jane's upper back with gentle strokes, almost like he doesn't know he's doing it. I bet he does. I bet he can't stand not to be touching her.

Sitting around the table like this with them feels important. It feels like a big deal.

Birthdays were a big deal at our house when I was growing up. I looked forward to them like I looked forward to summer vacation and weekends. Back then, it was easy. Everybody brought a dish to pass and filled the tables outside to overflowing. We filled up hundreds of water balloons and the twenty or so kids who were always in attendance would spend hours in battle.

This—the four of us and Paige—is quieter, but Emily's put just as much preparation into it. She made appetizer trays and grilled burgers and hot dogs. Beau and Jane brought even more balloons—a bunch of eight of them, plus a big Happy Birthday balloon floating in the center. It's filled with just as much love as any of the parties I went to as a kid. It's more poignant, somehow. It squeezes at my heart to watch it. To be here.

"One minute," Emily says. She steps into the house. Every muscle in my body wants to follow her.

Instead, I turn to Paige. "Show me that zip line again. Should we set it up a little later?"

Her eyes light up. "Yes! Not later. Now."

"Well, I don't—"

"Happy birthday," Emily says. She comes back out onto the patio, the cake balanced in her hands, the candles lit. "Ready? One, two, three—"

The birthday song rises above the table and my heart beats harder. That thing I said to Emily in Paris—about moving back to Eben Cape—I don't know if I meant it, back then. I was just floating the idea. Now, it seems real, and I can't explain it. My life is in LA. My job is in LA. All those auditions and meetings and lunches are what build my career. But as we sing to Paige, I remember the argument in my mind. Not everyone has to live in LA.

Why would I want to be anywhere but here?

I lift up my phone at the last second and take a photo of her blowing out the candles. Emily stands behind her, one hand on her ponytail and a pure, genuine smile on her face. The second it snaps onto my screen, I know I'm going to keep it forever.

Emily cuts the cake. Paige gets the piece with her name on it, even though it's in the middle. I get a corner piece with a delicate frosting balloon.

It's light, and sweet, and afterward Paige leaps out of her chair. "Zip line," she says, clapping her hands. "Uncle Beau. Uncle Mateo. Zip line. Zip line!"

Beau stands up and points at me. "Zip line."

"Well, when you say it like that, how can I refuse?"

Paige laughs and sprints over to a tree.

"We need a bigger one," I tell her.

She peers up at it. "Why? It looks big enough to hold me."

"How will I go on the zip line, then?"

A broad grin. "You can't go on the zip line. It's for kids."

I put on my best horrified face. "You're say-ing—that I can't go on the zip line? Ever?"

"Never," says Paige, but then she bursts out laughing.

I'm right, anyway. The tree was too small. We pick two trees that look like they could support the weight of two full-grown men, which is about the level of safety I want out of this zip-line thing. Beau drops one end by one tree, then paces over to the other. It comes up about three feet short.

"I don't think you have enough zip line there, buddy," I call to him.

He glares at me. "You don't?"

"No. I think you're pretty bad at measuring."

"You picked the tree." I can feel in the air how badly he wants to call me an asshole, but he won't, not in front of Paige.

"Pick another one over there. A closer one."

He puts one hand to his head. "How will I ever choose without you?"

I jog over and snatch the other part of the zip line out of his hands. "Shh. I'm here. I've got it. You can relax."

"I hate you."

"You're my best friend, Beau Rochester."

It takes a good fifteen minutes to satisfy Beau that the zip line is securely attached to the trees.

When we're done, he tosses me the handle. "Test it."

Paige is watching, blue eyes wide. "Test it for me?"

"Paige says I can't."

"Test it," Beau insists.

"What if I fall off? Will you catch me?"

He rolls his eyes. "Yes, Mateo. I will run alongside and spot you if that's what gives you the courage."

I look Paige in the eye. "One time," I promise. "For safety."

She narrows her eyes, considering. "One time," she agrees.

We've set it up for Paige to be able to use, so it's maybe not the best ride I'll ever take. All I know is that you don't waste permission once it's given. I hop on the zip line and soar down it, then ditch at the end and roll into the ground, then pop up with a smile on my face.

"You didn't really fall," Paige laughs. "You did that on purpose."

"It was a test to see if it worked."

"To see if you could fall? You don't know how to fall?"

"Of course I know how to fall. I've done stunt work." I send the seat zipping back toward Beau, who is still shaking his head as he catches it. "Your turn."

I thought Paige got all her shrieking out on Big Thunder Mountain. Turns out she has plenty left for the zip line. She grips it tight, and Beau and I send her back and forth while Emily takes pictures.

It's so goddamn wholesome that eventually I have to take a break. It reminds me of all the best parts of my childhood. It illustrates in living color that I could have this too, if I was willing to give up LA. But LA is more than a city. It's a career. It's an entire life I've built there. An image of me as more than the small-town boy from Maine.

"Beer," I call, sending Paige back to Beau to be my delivery person.

"This is a child," he says, catching her.

The cool air in Emily's kitchen balances out the heat from the sun and from all that nostalgia over childhood and fatherhood and everything else I have no business being nostalgic for. I take a chilled beer out of the fridge and open it. Needing a minute to lean against the countertop before I go back out there.

A neat stack of papers perches next to Emily's laptop on the kitchen counter. A printed version of her manuscript. It must be. She's only working on the one book, as far as I know, and that has to be it.

It's wrong to look at it.

Wrong to go and hover over the countertop.

Wrong to flip the first few pages.

I do it anyway.

My father was not a good boss. I've said it before, but it bears saying again. In a town like Eben Cape, the consequences of a person's actions are never fully contained. What my father did at the Eben Cape Canning Co. followed me to school.

Greg Molter's father worked for mine at the canning company. When Joe and I were relatively safe at home, Greg's dad was the one being bullied by my father.

You see how it happens.

At the end of the night, our father came home to us, and Greg's father came home to him. He let off steam to his wife. He let his hurt show on his face. He could do that at home. He couldn't do that at the canning company.

I don't blame Greg for how he felt. It must have seemed unthinkable to stand by and do nothing. Of course, Greg couldn't target my father. As an adult, and as his father's boss, my dad was completely out of his reach.

I wasn't.

He started small. Insults in the hallway. Pulling

my hair. Whenever Greg could find me, he retaliated. It got worse and worse until the day he waited for me after school.

Like all bullies, Greg attracted a crowd. He wasn't alone when he confronted me, spitting mad. I'll never forget how red his face was or how tightly clenched his fists were.

In my mind, I had nowhere to go. It didn't occur to me to go back into school. I was frozen with fear.

I was alone, and then I wasn't. Joe stepped out of the school. He took one look at Greg and his friends and put his body in front of mine.

"Emily," he said. "Run."

When he got home an hour later, his shirt was torn and he had a black eye that wouldn't fade for over a week.

"It's not so bad," he told me, and I was relieved, too. It was no worse than what our father would have done. I brought him a cloth for his bloody knuckles and frozen peas for his eye. I held it on for him.

"Thank you," I told my brother, there in the kitchen.

His eyes were closed. "Don't worry, Em. You're my sister. I'll always protect you."

I flip the pages shut and pace around the island, getting distance from the words on the page. I can't get any distance from the ache in my heart.

This has to be the hardest thing she's ever done. With the exception of being apart from Paige, what could be more difficult than loving her brother? He had turned into a monster, but he hadn't always been that way. Emily knew that. She lived it.

There were no big birthday parties, either. It was just the two of them and her asshole father. Her family's not much bigger now. She's got Beau and Jane and Paige, but—Christ. She's so alone. So brave in the face of all of this.

Emily comes in through the door, her hair windblown, balancing the half-eaten cake on one palm. She stops dead inside the door. Her eyes go down to the pages on the table. They're not perfect, the way they used to be.

"You shouldn't have read that." Tears spring to her eyes.

I could say that everybody's going to read it eventually, but I don't bother. I know better than that. I know I violated her privacy. I know I should feel remorse, feel like shit about it, but I don't.

I don't.

I want to understand Emily Rochester. I want to explore every dark shadow in her mind. To shine light in them. She steps up to the island and puts down the cake. A shuddering breath lifts her shoulders.

I abandon the beer and go to her.

As I fold my arms around her body, she reaches for me.

"You hate me," she says, trying to push me away even as she pulls me closer. I hold her tighter. There are no words of apology that would mean anything right now. No promises, either. But she's not going to stand there alone with tears in her eyes. Not while I'm in the room.

The other thing, my mind tells me. *Not hate. Love.* But I don't say it. It would only terrify Emily, a woman who's learned to fear the men who love her.

CHAPTER TWENTY-TWO

Jane Mendoza

HEAT FROM THE fire in Emily's outdoor fire ring plays across my face. The sun will be setting soon. It's getting late, but I can tell Paige doesn't want the party to end.

Who would? We've had a late lunch and hours on the zip line. Mateo sat in the grass with Paige and painted rocks. The two of them lined all the painted rocks up in a row and chose favorites, then chose again. Emily got out a frisbee and we all took turns tossing it to one another across the yard.

I'm surprised at how little awkwardness there is. I'd expected some between Mateo and Emily. They both came out of the kitchen a while back looking secretive. I don't know what they could be hiding. Mateo took her to Paris. It wouldn't be the biggest leap for them to just… be together.

It would be strange, for sure. Mateo didn't trust Emily when she made her return. He didn't want things to be harder for Beau. But now…

No awkwardness.

Nobody's in any hurry to leave, either. I didn't attend many birthday parties growing up in Houston, but when I did, they were a rushed madhouse. Nobody's mother seemed very happy to be hosting. Somehow, there was never enough food for the guests. Or maybe I just remember it that way.

This party's different. It's far closer to the parties I imagined for the nice families. The ones with money, and spare time. The ones who weren't hurrying to get it over with so they could work a night shift at the hospital or the factory.

The four of us and Paige make a nice family. I don't know how to classify what Beau and I are to Paige now. Technically, he's her uncle, but since we're not married, I'm just the former nanny.

But out here, gathered near Emily's patio, the labels don't seem to matter much at all. They're just not very accurate. "Paige's uncle" doesn't encompass the fact that Beau was her only parent for months. It doesn't encompass the way we live right next door to them. The way she goes between houses like she knows she belongs in both.

Family is the only word we have.

"Do you have enough marshmallows?" Emily asks. She's just come out from the kitchen with graham crackers and a package of Hershey bars.

"We can only roast one at a time," says Beau. "I think we're covered unless you want to put twenty on a stick and do them all at once." Mateo starts to get up. "Oh, sit down. It was a joke."

Mateo sits back in his seat with a grin, but his eyes go to Emily. They follow her as she takes the seat next to me. It's hard to tell through the curls of heat in the air, but I think his hand tightens on the neck of his beer bottle. Like he wants to be touching her.

"I bet Paige is going to crash tonight," Emily murmurs to me. "She has to be getting so tired."

"It's been a good party. Non-stop action. And the cake was beautiful."

Her cheeks pinken at the compliment. "Thank you. I thought about going to a bakery, but I didn't want…" Emily trails off. "I decided to keep things private. Adding all those little decorations with the frosting is kind of like meditating, anyway. Can't focus on anything else."

"It turned out so well."

"Maybe that's what I'll be in my next life. A cake decorator." Emily looks at Paige, at the fire. A quick glance at Mateo, but then she looks away again. "I don't know if I'd want to do wedding cakes, though. That seems like a lot of pressure."

My heart aches for her. I know Emily doesn't mind making her daughter's birthday cake. I know she'd do it again, every year if that's what Paige wanted. I just wish the stress was over for her. I wish she could go down to the bakery in Eben Cape without worrying about photographers or rumors or God knows what else. We're relatively safe here, behind all the security that Mateo hired, but…

But.

How long can you stay confined? How long could Emily? We're not close enough for me to ask her, but I wonder about it anyway. Does it ever feel like hiding?

If it does, I hope it's not bothering her tonight. Trouble seems farther away, at least to me.

Paige stands next to the fire with Beau by her side. She holds a marshmallow on a stick.

"Keep turning it." Beau keeps his hands over hers. "Slowly. Evenly."

"What happens if I do it fast?"

"Maybe nothing. Or maybe it slips a little and

catches on fire."

Paige's eyes get wide, and then she focuses harder on the marshmallow.

"That wouldn't be the worst thing," offers Mateo. "I like burnt marshmallows."

Paige wrinkles her nose. "You do?"

"If you cover them in chocolate, you barely taste the scorched parts."

"But if it did light on fire, what would we do?" My heart beats a little faster at her question. Coach House started burning while Beau and Paige and I were asleep.

Beau puts a hand on her back. "If a marshmallow catches on fire, it's pretty easy to blow out. Like a candle."

This seems to satisfy Paige. "Jane." She says my name without looking at me. "Do you like my new zip line?"

"It looks like so much fun. All of your presents look amazing."

"They are amazing." Her voice turns slightly wistful. "This is the best day ever. I wish we could do this every day."

"This is the best day for sure." Mateo stretches his legs in front of him and drinks from his beer. "I've never seen a zip line set up more professionally than yours."

"All thanks to you," says Beau. "Never would have managed if you weren't here, Mateo."

"How does it feel to be eight years old?"

She thinks about it. The breeze rustles her hair and sends the scent of the fire wafting over to me. That smell, over new green grass and the sea, seems like the kind of thing they could make into a candle. Summer in Maine. But then, it could be different in other parts of Maine. Summer in Eben Cape.

"The same," Paige says finally. "But I have more presents now."

"What's your favorite gift?"

"I loved the bracelet from you guys." No hesitation. She already knows. I wonder if she and Mateo talked about favorite presents while they lined up all those rocks. "And I love the zip line from Mom. And I loved the new Nintendo Switch from Uncle Mateo." Paige cocks her head to the side as she twists the marshmallow stick with great care, like Beau told her. "The present from Uncle Joe was nice, too."

I freeze. My blood freezes. Everything freezes. I feel Emily stiffen next to me. Across the fire, Mateo frowns. Beau concentrates on the fire, but his shoulders go up. A present from Joe shouldn't be possible. I can't fathom how he would have brought her a gift for her birthday.

"What present was that again?" I hope my voice sounds as casual as I meant it to.

Paige doesn't seem to notice. "Yeah, he sent it to me. I don't know how, though. But the envelope had my name on it. *Paige Rochester.* Do you think they have a post office in jail? They probably have one if he sent it to me."

"I don't think I saw that one." I let a few beats pass. "Can you show me?"

"It's that one on top." Paige doesn't look toward the patio table. "The wooden one. I don't want to burn this marshmallow. I think it's turning out good."

The wooden carving is on the top of all Paige's other gifts and the box the zip line came in. Joe—or someone else, I guess—whittled it into its current shape. It's clearly the top hat from Monopoly. Paige picks the top hat more than any other piece.

"Would you look at that?" I stand up and cross over to the table. A folded note has been discarded near the hat. I pick it up with two fingers, only to realize I'm being ridiculous. The paper won't scream at me, or burst into flame. It won't threaten me with an investigation. It won't summon Joe's presence to the party.

It's just a note that says *J.*

Beside it, there's a manila envelope with scrawled handwriting. Sure enough, it's addressed to Paige Rochester with the address of the Coach House.

"Emily, could you come here a second? I have a quick question." Emily smiles at Paige as she gets out of her seat. Paige isn't even looking. I'm grateful for her concentration now. Grateful that she wants this single marshmallow to be the most perfect marshmallow in history. Grateful for Beau, who hasn't let on that there's any problem. Emily gets closer, and I hold up the note. "Did you see this?"

"No." Fear flashes in her eyes. "I brought the mail inside earlier. She must have looked through the stack. If it was addressed to her she would have opened it."

I shiver. It feels like Joe has infiltrated the party, even though I know he's in jail. He might have friends who are still on the force, but they're not going to let him walk free to do this. Goose bumps fan out on my shoulders. We have plenty of security. There's no need to feel like he's sneaking around in the woods, hovering just out of sight.

Emily takes the envelope from my hand and

turns it right-side up. "This isn't his handwriting." She keeps her voice low so there's no chance it carries. A shiver moves down my spine.

"It's not?"

"No." Emily traces the letter on the page as if to verify for herself that it's really not her brother's handwriting. "No, it's definitely not. Someone else wrote this."

"Do you still think this gift was from him?"

Emily looks over her shoulder and scans across the entire yard. Now that she's done it, I take my own turn checking behind my back. There's no one in Emily's kitchen. Joe isn't standing at the patio door with a crazed look in his eyes. The expensive security didn't let him slip past, and neither did the warden at the jail. I remember how haunted Emily looked when I first met her. How desperate. She'd followed me to Houston in a bid to get her daughter back, and this note, this gift—it's brought back an element of that haunting.

"Okay," Emily says softly. She closes her eyes and takes a few deep breaths. "Okay. Yes. I think this gift is from him. He knows when Paige's birthday is, and he knows enough about her to send it. But he's obviously covering his tracks."

"What do you mean? He left a note." Or he

instructed someone else to leave the note.

"A note that's not his handwriting," Emily points out. "He wants us to know it was him, but he still has plausible deniability. It would be hard to trace this back to him."

We both look at the top hat. It's small and unassuming and a little bit cute.

My heart thunders, but I force myself to analyze it like I'm someone who's not at the party. Who hasn't been threatened by Joe Causey. By someone who's not afraid.

"It's not a terrible gift," I admit to Emily. "It's something she likes. And obviously crafted. That takes time."

"It's proof."

Beau's voice floats to us from over by the fire. "I've never seen a more perfect marshmallow."

Paige giggles. "Are you serious?"

"I'm serious. Put it right here on the chocolate, and then you can eat it."

"Proof that he's still thinking about you?" I ask the question, but I don't really want to know the answer. I don't want Joe to have sent anything to Paige in the first place.

"Proof that he can get to my daughter even when he's in jail," Emily says softly. "It's not a gift. It's a threat."

CHAPTER TWENTY-THREE

Beau Rochester

HOW THE HELL did Joe Causey send Paige a gift?

Well, I know how. We've tracked the package through the post office. It was dropped off at a blue container in a remote part of town. The return address is bogus. The handwriting doesn't match Joe's. There's no way to pin it on him, but we know he's behind it.

I don't like it. I don't like any damn thing about it. Mateo and I both sent a string of text messages after Emily showed us the note. His were probably more charming than mine. I'm pissed. Nothing from Joe should have gotten through to Paige's birthday party.

I pace the first floor of the house, checking the locks on the doors and windows. Lights glow in the windows up at Emily's. We're both still awake, or she's leaving them on tonight.

The cliff is locked up tight. I know that. Drones are the only things that can get up here, and nobody's tried that yet, far as I know. It doesn't make me feel any more relaxed.

I send another text to Liam North.

Beau: *Anything?*

He's quick on the draw.

Liam: *No. I added people at the access road and up by the houses. Nothing's getting through.*

I check the locks one more time. The house doesn't have bulletproof windows, but it does have a security system that will cause a hell of a racket if somebody breaks one of them.

One more loop to turn off the lights, and I climb the stairs to the second floor. The boards have no give. They're all brand-new. Coach House made constant noise. Old houses like that are always complaining. I wouldn't mind the warning now, but we're not in Coach House anymore. We're in our new life.

New life, old ghosts. Joe Causey's still hovering over everything, that bastard.

The bedroom door opens without a sound.

Jane's already in here. Tucked in bed. Freshly showered, the scent of her shampoo in the air. She's under the covers, a book propped on her knees.

I was wrong. Joe Causey can't hover over this moment. It's all mine.

Jane looks up from her book and smiles. She's so goddamn beautiful. It's a cliché to say a person is beautiful inside and out, but with Jane, it's true. I feel guilt and hunger every time she smiles at me like this. Guilt that I'm ruining her. Sapping her of her innate goodness. And hunger that I'll never be able to satiate. Not even if I live forever.

"Everything safe downstairs?" she teases, and I hear the real worry below her tone.

"Downstairs and everywhere else."

She lets out a breath. "Good. I want Emily to be okay tonight. She put all that work into the party."

I want to climb into the bed and never get out, but I force myself to be a civilized person. "Don't go anywhere," I tell her on the way past. It feels good to shed my jeans and get a fresh T-shirt. Better to brush my teeth. That damn gift left a sour taste in my mouth. It shouldn't have happened. If I'm honest, none of this should have happened. I should never have fucked the nanny.

It's possible I shouldn't have hired a nanny in the first place. I shouldn't have let things go so far with Emily and Rhys.

But I rinse away these objections. Whether I should or shouldn't have is irrelevant now. I did all those things, and we're in this place.

I can't even say that I'd do them differently. That probably makes me a selfish bastard, but I wouldn't. Every step I took brought me to Jane Mendoza. Well—it brought her to me, delivered to my doorstep in the pouring rain.

Back in the bedroom, I turn off the lights, leaving us with her bedside lamp. Jane puts aside her book as I climb into bed and take her in my arms.

We breathe like that for several minutes.

I made a fortune on the West Coast. More money than I knew what to do with. I had the idea that it would make things easier. I'd go back to Emily and give her the kind of life she deserved. I'd buy myself that life.

I believed it was something for sale.

But all the money in the world couldn't have conjured Jane Mendoza into being. Once she was in my life, I couldn't buy her heart.

Love doesn't have a price tag.

And this—holding her in my arms, feeling her

225

warmth, the way her body settles into mine? There's nothing I wouldn't pay.

Jane reaches to the bedside table. I keep a hand on her belly as she stretches just to feel her move. The switch clicks. The room falls into darkness. Then she returns my arms, burrowing down into the bed, under the covers.

"So." Her voice is sweet. I know what she's going to ask me about. I wish this was over, so she didn't have to ask me about it ever again. "What happened?"

"A lot of calls and texts."

"Who'd you call?"

"Everyone. The cops. The prosecutor. The FBI. Every contact I had in my phone."

"And?"

"And nothing." Frustration wells. "They can't link it to him."

"It is linked to him, though. There was a note that said his name."

"Anyone could have written that note." I run my fingers through her hair. I don't know how she gets it to be so silky all the damn time.

Jane sighs. "That's what Emily was afraid of. She said he would have plausible deniability."

"She was right."

"I hate that for her." Jane shifts against me,

resting her head against my chest. "I was hoping she'd be wrong."

"We were all hoping she'd be wrong." I let myself hope for that, too. Some easy, simple link between Joe and the carving.

"It's just so much." I can feel Jane's sympathy in every word. Her empathy. "Emily knew what she was risking to come back here and fight for Paige. She knew Joe would be dangerous, and he was. I wish the world would let up."

"I wish Joe would let up."

"Everybody thinks it was him, then?"

"Until we know otherwise, yes. The Monopoly piece is Paige's favorite. She's liked the top hat since before she knew how to play the game. Joe would know that kind of thing."

"But if someone else did know…"

A laugh escapes. A frustrated one. "That person would have had to go to a lot of trouble to set him up. And for what? A birthday gift to his niece? He can always argue that he didn't mean for it to be intimidating. No, it was him. He didn't write the note or get it here, but it was him."

Jane's quiet. She's quiet for so long that I run a hand up and down her back. If she's asleep, I'll let her be. But she stirs again, brushing a lock of hair away from her face.

"How does this stop, then?"

"A conviction."

"He's already in jail."

"He's being held in the county jail. If he's convicted, they'll move him somewhere else. Somewhere maximum security, I'd bet."

"Then…" Jane lifts her head to kiss the line of my jaw. "I have to testify."

"No, you don't."

"Yes, I do. He came after me, and he came after Emily. If I stay silent, I'm letting him off the hook."

I take her face in my hand and find her lips. Kiss her. "He's not off the hook. He's in jail."

"You just said that the only way to make this stop was a conviction." Jane's voice heats, and I'm instantly rock hard. Her sweetness gets me that way. So does her passion. "I'm not leaving a single thing on the table."

"It's a risk."

"How so?"

"Because if they don't convict and that bastard walks free, he'll know what you said about him. You'd be putting yourself on the line for a chance to make Emily's life easier."

"It would also be a chance to make Paige's life

easier." Jane winds one of her legs around mine, pressing her body in close. "Damn it, Jane. Why can't you make my life easier instead?"

"How would I do that?" I can't take it. The innocent tone. The sweet voice in my ear. "Tell me. I'll do anything to make you feel better."

"Come here." I pull her on top of me and settle her thighs over my hips. "You don't have to testify. I don't want you in any more danger than you already have been."

"I'm not worried about it."

"This isn't making my life easier, sweetheart."

It's a half-truth. Having her with me like this is a hell of a lot easier than being alone.

"Why would I worry about it when I have you to protect me?"

"Because I'm a goddamn human. It's possible for me to fuck up. I've done it before with you. And you're going to sit here and tell me it's okay for you to testify? It's not just Joe."

"I know," she says. "It's the whole police department. It's any of those guys who still worship him." Jane rocks her hips. She's fighting dirty. It's a damn good way to win this argument. "But if nobody speaks up, they just get to keep doing what they're doing. How is that better?"

I put my hands on her waist. Her curves under my palms wipe out most of my critical thinking abilities. "I want what's better for you. I don't give a shit about dirty cops."

"Yes, you do."

"Not right now I don't."

"Then stop fighting with me."

"I'm not fighting with you. I'm telling you not to testify."

"And I'm telling you that I'm going to testify. For Emily. For Paige. For every woman in this town who's had a bad experience with one of those officers. You're not going to let them get to me."

I want to believe that. I want to believe the walls of our house are solid steel. That the windows can't be shattered. I want to believe that my love for her can keep all the bastards of the world from even looking in her direction. But the world doesn't work that way.

"You ever think I'm the one you should worry about? I'm already here with you, Jane Mendoza. I've already gotten to you."

"Yeah." This breathy agreement makes me want to pin her to the bed and keep her there for the rest of her life. "You did. We could keep talking about it, or you could just accept that you've won."

"How's that? You won't agree to stay safe."

"I'll agree to stay with you," Jane points out, bending low to kiss me again. "In this house you built for me. In this bed."

"College," I manage to say, but barely. "You have to go to college, damn it."

"We can talk about that another time," she whispers.

I should be a better man. I know that. I should sit her down and make her understand how serious I am about her safety. About her life. I should look her in those big, dark eyes and keep talking until she hears every word I'm saying. Until she knows that putting herself at risk isn't tolerable for me. Not on this level. What the hell would I do if something happened to her? How would I go on? I used to think I could do it, but having Paige in my life, and having Jane—it's made me more aware of my own limitations. I can't live without Jane Mendoza.

But I can't say that to her, because I'm not a better man. I want to kiss her and hold her tight against me until she's squirming with frustration. I want to make her come so hard she can't stay awake after. I want all those things and more, and I want them tonight.

"This isn't over," I tell her. All I can do before

I roll us over.

"I know," Jane whispers, and then we're all done talking for the night.

CHAPTER TWENTY-FOUR

Emily Rochester

*E*VERYONE IN SCHOOL *wanted to date Beau Rochester. Girls doodled his name in their notebooks. They stole looks at him in the hallway. Is it any surprise that I wanted to date him, too? I tried not to want that. I tried to be the kind of girl who didn't care about whether that boy with the dark hair and deep gray eyes knew who I was.*

It didn't stop me from getting a crush on him. I looked for him in the hall between classes. When we had one together, I kept constant track of where he was in the room. And when he asked me out, I said yes.

Dating was public in Eben Cape. There weren't too many people in school, so there was no such thing as a secret boyfriend. If you went out to the local burger place with a guy, everyone knew about it.

So everyone knew when I started dating Beau.

I found myself drawn to his intensity. I wanted

to be the girl who finally made him open up. I really wanted to know what it would take to make him laugh. The more he withheld from me, the more I wanted from him. I made it my project. I asked him questions about himself. I listened carefully to the answers. And I was always available when he wanted to see me.

It took Beau a few months to invite me to his house. We went after school and spent half an hour pretending to do our homework at the kitchen table. He had just suggested a walk on the beach when his older brother Rhys got home.

Rhys, like Beau, was handsome. Unlike Beau, he seemed more open. He had an easier smile, and he strode across the kitchen to shake my hand with a grin on his face. He asked me questions about myself. About school. About my friends. The kinds of questions that came harder to Beau.

At some point, Beau went through into the next room. For what, I don't know. His shoes? To keep himself from snapping at his brother? Either way, I was alone with Rhys.

"You're pretty," he said, and he stepped closer. "You look like you'd be a good kisser."

"I am," I said. I was being bold because I couldn't be any other way. Rhys took up the whole room with his presence.

I meant to say more, but he got there first.

"Prove it." His grin never faltered. "Come out with me on Friday night."

"What?" My face went hot, my bravado fading away. "I'm here with Beau. He's your brother."

"So?" he said.

I should have known then what he was. A creep. Worse than a creep. The man who would turn my existence into a living hell.

I toss the pen down next to the notepad. Sometimes I type on the computer, but this—this I've been writing by hand while Paige naps on the couch. She went back and forth on her zip line for hours this morning, sprawled out on the cushions, and went out. I haven't seen her nap like this since she was a toddler.

I'm glad to have her close. I'm glad she didn't go upstairs to her room. It's hard to let Paige out of my sight after everything that's happened. It was difficult when I first came back to her, but now? After that gift at the party?

God.

Joe meant it as a threat. I don't believe for an instant that it was an overture. Or a peace offering. I don't think he's been capable of that kind of gesture for years. I don't expect for him to change his ways. It's sad to accept that about my own brother. It hurts more than I thought, to be this resigned about Joe.

I wish things had turned out differently.

A security guard passes by the kitchen window and gives me a little wave. They're more visible now. Closer to the house than ever. I feel some relief, of course—it's good to know they're there. But then, Joe got past them by mailing something.

I rub my hands over my face. He mailed her a gift. That doesn't mean he could actually hurt Paige.

Could he?

I shiver at the thought. Paige stirs as if she felt it, too. She slides off the couch and pads over to me, rubbing her eyes. My daughter drops her head onto my shoulder. She's warm and sleepy, and it reminds me so much of when she was little that my heart squeezes at the memory.

"Mommy," she says, her voice soft like it's the middle of the night instead of the middle of the afternoon. I used to love the whispered, almost nonsensical conversations we'd have after she woke up from her afternoon naps. Back when she'd just started talking, she would talk and talk and I never understood a word. You pretend, though. You have a full conversation and all that matters is that you were talking to each other.

"Yes?" I rub her back. You never know when your child is going to stop napping. One day they just refuse, and you don't have a toddler you can tuck into a crib anymore. You don't have those hour-long stretches of peace in the afternoon. I used to crave Paige's naptime, and then miss her when she was asleep. By the time I heard her babbling in her crib, I'd feel almost giddy at going to get her out again. Paige with her blonde bedhead and her chubby hands.

"I remember when you and Daddy would fight."

I want to back away from the topic. I want to tiptoe away. Offer her some distraction, the way I would do when she was small and upset. But I won't invalidate her memories that way. I won't pretend it didn't happen. My heart races against my will.

"I remember that, too." Her arms tighten around my neck. More of her weight is settling into my lap. Another instinct—to overexplain. To keep talking until I've covered over the past with my words. I want to move us into the future, assure her that it won't happen again. That's a promise I can keep. I will never fight with her father again. He'll never hit me again. He'll never touch me again.

I don't say those things, either.

I wait. I hope I'm projecting calm. Giving her the impression that this is a space to share her feelings. No matter how much I wish we could both forget.

"He would shout. He had a loud voice."

Even louder when you stood in the same room, the way I did. "He used a very loud voice."

The word choice seems important right now. Rhys chose to be loud and intimidating. He wasn't always that way. Like most people, he had the capability to speak in a level tone. That's not how he chose to be when he was angry. I could see him deciding to get louder. I've heard people describe angry men as "losing control," but that's not what happened with Rhys. If he apologized at all, he would use that excuse, too. It was a lie. He knew what he was doing. He felt entitled to violence. It was no loss of control.

"I remember," Paige begins again. "I remember that I would stay in my room. You said that I should stay in my room until you came to get me."

"I did say that."

"Why?" She turns her head and rubs her face into my shoulder, then rests again. "Why did you say I should stay in there? Stay in there and stay quiet," she murmurs, almost to herself.

I can still taste those words on my tongue, and the desperation that came along with them. How do you communicate to a child that it's very, very serious, that it could be life or death? You can't. I couldn't. I had to pray that Paige understood, on some level, that our safety depended on her staying put. I feel so damn guilty about it. That old guilt makes my throat tight.

It was always a choice I had to make. I never had the blind courage to take Paige and run. Rhys was the kind of man who wouldn't take no for an answer. He wouldn't stop for anything. And I knew the stats as well as any other woman. I knew that my life would be in the most danger at the very moment I tried to leave. I used to lay awake nights, Rhys next to me in the bed, and make lists in my head. Places he would be least likely to find us. Places he wouldn't think to look. Places he hated, so he'd never search there. Places he loved, so he'd assume I went elsewhere.

And if we were in hiding, we'd need a plan for making it work long-term. We'd have to change our appearance. Change our names. It was a different world already than the one I grew up in. Everyone has a smartphone with a high-definition camera. Anyone could take our photo and post it on the internet. Living off the grid with a child didn't seem like a real option. Where would she go to school? How would she find friends? I knew I wouldn't be enough for her. Not forever. But if we ran, other people would always be a danger to us.

So I didn't run.

I told Paige to hide instead. I held both her hands and looked into her eyes and told her to hide.

"I thought it would be better," I finally say. "That's why I did that. I'm sorry I asked you to do that. I'm sorry I had to ask you."

"It's not your fault," she answers with a yawn, and the words shock me. Not my fault. The things Rhys did weren't my fault, but choosing to stay? I bear at least some responsibility for that. "Daddy hurt you, but you protected me. Didn't you?"

"I tried my best." My love and guilt and sadness and pride threaten my voice. They make it something small. "I tried to keep you away from that."

"That's why you didn't want me to make a sound. So he would hit you instead of me."

I can't speak. My heart is breaking. It's already broken, but it breaks again. I gather her into my arms and smooth her curls. She's right. I was trying to keep her from the sound, of course. I tried to keep him calm for as long as I could. But in the end, at the heart of it—I wanted him to go after me. Tire himself out on me.

The guilt I feel about all those harried, whispered conversations about staying in her room and staying quiet is nothing compared to how I would feel if he'd hurt her.

There's no way to put that into words. Not now. Not today. Paige has already seen too much for a person so young, and I just can't. I'm just going to sit in this moment for her while she wakes up from her nap.

I'm just going to be with her.

It hurts to think about these things she remembers, but it hurts less than remembering them when we were apart. That was the worst pain I've ever felt.

It's over, I remind myself. It's over. We're together. Whatever happens with Joe, whatever happens for the rest of our lives, we're together now.

Safe. Together. Now.

Afternoon sun filters in through the window. The house is new and alive around us. The near-silent central air keeps the rooms fresh. Another security guard will be by in a few minutes, but I don't let myself think of that. I concentrate on each breath. Mine and Paige's. Hers are steady and sleepy. Mine are slightly jagged. I make mine match hers.

We're okay.

We're going to be okay.

CHAPTER TWENTY-FIVE

Mateo Garza

CATRINA GONZALES IS not happy with me. She sighs deeply over the phone, the sound of traffic in the background. Probably out on the sidewalk in front of some restaurant. Probably in the middle of a high-powered dinner.

"The deal isn't going to be on the table forever, Mateo. This is everything you were hoping for, and it's not going to wait around for you to—"

"The deal's not on the table at all." We've gone around in this circle for five minutes already. Enough. "I'm not taking this deal or any other deal. I'm on personal leave."

"Jesus," she hisses. "This could be it for you. Do you understand what I'm saying? This is the kind of thing that could tank your career. Not just this movie. The entire thing. You turn down this offer, word's going to get around that you're not dedicated. No second chances."

"That's fine."

"Mateo—"

"Catrina, I'm on leave. I have things going on. I'll talk to you when I have something new to share."

In the split second of silence that follows I end the call and toss my phone onto the passenger seat. It's nine in LA. Midnight on the East Coast. And I'm almost at Emily's house. I've been waved through three separate security stops on the way up the road. I'm going to see her.

I need to see her.

There's a light in the living room as I pull up to the house, but Emily's not inside. She's out on the porch with her phone. The screen illuminates her face. My headlights skim across the front porch and I shut them off. Turn the key in the ignition. Climb out of the car.

Emily sits on a wicker love seat, a blanket over her lap, her phone in her hand. "I could have been asleep," she says as I step onto the porch.

"You weren't asleep." I knew she wouldn't be. I can't say how. It's like I felt her across Eben Cape, being awake in the night.

"What are you doing here?"

I did this once before when she was staying in

that shitty A-frame with no insulation. Showed up at the house at night and questioned her about her intentions with Beau and Paige. I have questions now. They're not about her intentions.

"I thought you might want company."

The smallest smile curves the corner of her lips. "Can I trust you to be good company?"

Yes. "I took you to Disneyland Paris."

"I slept in your bed in the hotel."

"You trusted me then."

She studies me. "I guess I can trust you in Eben Cape, too." The night sounds at Emily's house are different. The crickets make a racket. The roll of the sea is louder. "Do you want to come inside?"

I should have a response to this. A slick comeback that will play off her invitation. But it's late, and I've wanted to be back at Emily's house since I woke up this morning.

"Yes."

Emily stands up, gathering the blanket into her arms, and leads the way inside. "Paige is sleeping," she says, locking the door behind us. Emily taps at the buttons on her security system. A light blinks. She looks into my eyes. I would give anything to know what she's thinking right now. "Let's go upstairs."

Upstairs to her master bedroom. Upstairs to a space that is all Emily. Crisp neutrals. Beautiful little details. Small flourishes of color. I close the door. Lock it. When I turn back to her, she's standing in the center of the room.

"What are you doing here?" she asks again.

"You slept in my bed in Paris."

Her cheeks flush. "Yeah. And?"

"And I didn't kiss you."

"I fell asleep."

"It was an oversight. I wanted to."

Emily takes in the space between us. The air is charged. Almost thick with feeling. "Then why aren't you kissing me now? You've done it before."

"I want to do more than kiss you."

"You're here at midnight, Mateo. If you wanted to sleep with me—"

"I do." Nothing but honesty now, for Christ's sake. "But that's not why I came here. I came here to keep you company."

"You came here in the middle of the night to not sleep with me." Even her skepticism is captivating.

"I don't want to hurt you."

"Feelings aren't permanent." Emily lifts her chin. "They don't last forever."

✧　✧　✧

Emily Rochester

MATEO LAUGHS. HUFFS, really. Self-deprecating and charming. I feel like my heart might beat itself out of commission.

"Not like that," he says. "Physically."

"Why would you—"

He meets my eyes, lust heavy in his gaze. "I like it rough, sweetheart. And you've been through enough."

Part of me rears back and gets ready to run. Part of me screams to abort this mission. The alarm sounds like an endless refrain of haven't you learned your lesson?

Another part of me is curious. Alive and electric with what Mateo's just said to me. It seems… completely at odds with the person I know him to be. Rough? But he's not like Rhys or like my father. It must mean something other than cruel violence.

"Show me."

"No."

"Yes," I demand. "I invited you in. And now I want you to show me what you mean."

He looks off to the side—a moment of indecision—but then he's crossing the room. Then he's close enough to touch me. Mateo's fingers graze the sides of my neck and slip lower. He circles one of my wrists with a fingertip. He's being incredibly gentle.

And then he takes both of my wrists and pins them behind my back. It's not a particularly violent movement but I gasp anyway. This is a loss of control. It makes me shiver. Mateo uses his other hand to tip my chin up so he can look into my eyes.

"Okay?" he says.

I nod, but he keeps watching. My breathing, I think. He wants to make sure I'm not hyperventilating. Not afraid.

I am afraid. But it's the kind that heats my skin and makes my thighs press together. The length of my spine feels molten.

Mateo dips his head to the side of my neck. Soft kisses. They're a distraction. He's moving us. Pushing and pushing and pushing until we're at the wall. At the last moment, he changes the position of my wrists. Pins them above my head. He's never used his strength like this with me before, and it takes a lot of effort to keep my breath from becoming too shallow.

I don't want him to stop.

Mateo pushes a knee between my legs, and my mind collapses down onto the pressure. His solid thigh. My softest parts. We're both fully clothed but I feel naked. Completely exposed.

He kisses the side of my neck again. My jaw. Below my ear. "I could hold you like this while I fucked you." His voice sends more heat rushing through my body. "Pin you. I think you'd like that. A thick cock taking your pussy while you couldn't move. See? You're already trying to get it." Shame bleeds into my desire. I don't think I could stop moving my hips if I wanted to. I just need more friction. I need more. All the pent-up need I've had for years is out in the open now. "Emily Rochester, fucking my thigh. Ride harder. Ride like you imagine I'll fuck you."

I can't help it. Every word he says is like a spell. It compels movement. I have to do it. I wanted him to come over, and he did. I wanted him to show me what he likes. And he did. This is only a hint of what he'd do with me, and it lit me on fire. It's hard to do this with my wrists pinned. He knows that. He likes that. Mateo holds my wrists tighter to the wall and looks down at my body, working over his.

"Goddamn," he murmurs. "You want this. I can feel how hot you are through your clothes."

He's not going anywhere. It's a heady, almost drunken feeling, how strong he is. I could grind myself against his thigh all night and he wouldn't move. I could do it for weeks. For years. I don't have to be strong right now. He can do it.

"That sound," he groans. "Make that noise again."

I do it, helpless and hungry. I haven't done this in a long time. I haven't wanted to do this with anyone in a long time. And this is dirty, and yet somehow playful.

Somehow it's everything I've wanted.

"You're going to come," he says, his voice low.

"No." I feel frantic about it. One moment, it's fine, the next moment—I don't know. I don't know. "I can't."

"Yes, you can. Let it happen, Emily. I'll be here when it's over."

I can't resist. It happens almost without my permission. A wave of pleasure so strong it knocks me into him.

"Gorgeous," Mateo says. "Look at you. I've never seen anyone look so pretty when they come. Don't stop yet. Let me see your face." I look into his eyes. It's the one thing I can bring myself to do. He curses under his breath. "So goddamn beautiful. Let me fuck you."

I can't get the word *yes* out through the shudder of my orgasm and so I end up nodding. I must look ridiculous but I can't do it less enthusiastically than I am. Mateo takes me from the wall, takes me to my bed, and strips off my clothes while I stand at the side.

Then he bends me over it and unzips his pants.

I'm panting with need for him. Actually panting. It's not like me. It *could* be what I'm like if Mateo was always here, but we can't get into that.

This is about sex. Not about tomorrow or the next day. Not about forever.

He pushes into me. Firm. Unyielding.

I understand, in a distant sort of way, that he's being as patient as he can. He's taking as much as he can for himself without hurting me. Much, anyway. There's still an element of pain. There's still an element of stretch.

It's hot.

I'd forgotten how good it could be. I'd forgotten how breathtaking and filthy it could feel to give my body to another person. I'd forgotten that a man could move this way. It's rough, but it's not violent. And I'm so wet for him. I wanted him. I wanted this.

Mateo's body comes down over mine, holding me at different points. Pinning me, like he said he would. But I can still breathe. It's not a fight to the death the way it was with Rhys. It's not a fight for anything. He's taking, and I'm getting.

"You feel so goddamn good," he says, and it shocks me that he could sound breathless and surprised. "You're going to make me come. Hold on tight. Can't stop."

He can't stop. The force of his body increases until I really do have to hold on for dear life. Until he's coming so hard he's speechless except for a few words. *Yes* and *Emily* and *so good.*

It's the closest we've ever been. It's the most I've ever seen him lose control. He pulls out of me and picks me up, taking us both to the bed. Mateo's breathing hard. I'm breathing harder. He leans down to kiss my collarbone. "Damn it, Emily. I love you."

It's like ice injected directly into my muscles. Retreat, that alarm in my head says. *Get away. Get away. Get away.* Love leads to things like a bad marriage.

Like broken promises. Like black eyes. *No. I can't. No.*

Mateo reaches for me, and I flinch. It's an instinctive reaction. I'm an animal cowering in that moment. My heart pounds. Fear doesn't let me distinguish between good men and bad men. There are only men, and their power over me.

Concern flashes into his eyes. Regret. "Emily—"

"Please leave." It's a struggle for the word, and once I've said it, the pain in Mateo's eyes is its own punishment. "Go. I need you to go."

"I don't have anywhere to be. Emily, it's all right. Let me—"

"No." I scramble out from underneath him and get to the other side of the bed. It doesn't feel good to be naked now. It feels awful and vulnerable and cold. I want walls between me and Mateo. Locks and walls. I want to be hidden from view. "Please leave."

He's stunned. I hate it. I hate the hurt in his eyes and the slope of his shoulders as he puts his clothes back in place.

"Are you sure?"

No. Stay.

"Please get out," I whisper. "Please."

He goes, and I stand at the window and watch his car until he's out of sight.

CHAPTER TWENTY-SIX

Jane Mendoza

THE COURTROOM IS small, which makes sense because Eben Cape is a small town.

Now it's filled to the brim. The media has latched onto this case with all its teeth. The seats are packed with men and women writing notes. They aren't allowed to bring cameras and microphones inside, but that doesn't stop them from reporting word for word.

I have a seat in the front row, beside Beau.

Wood paneling designed to make the room look distinguished mixes with cheap ceiling tiles and the faint smell of cleaning supplies. As I'm looking around I catch a man sketching me. The woman on the page looks solemn and slightly afraid.

I quickly turn away from him.

Beau takes my hand and squeezes.

He's not happy I'm here. Things have been tense between us since I agreed to testify, but he appeared outside the SUV when it was time to go.

Even though he hates this, he won't let me face it alone.

The judge is a black man with a permanent scowl. He presides over the proceedings with very little patience. I'm not sure if that works in our favor or against it. Probably both, at times.

Lauren Michaels stands up. "Your Honor, I call witness Jane Mendoza to the stand."

A trembling starts deep in my stomach. I feel like I'm about to throw up. Confrontation has always scared me, but this is escalated to a thousand. Especially when he nods, and Lauren gestures me forward. Beau squeezes one more time and then releases my hand.

I step through the wooden gate that divides the court from the audience. Part of me wants to lower my eyes. I don't want to meet the gaze of the judge or the jury. And I especially don't want to see Joe Causey, even though I can feel his dark gaze on me. I saw the back of him when we walked in. He looks crisp and clean-cut in a suit. The kind of man who inspired trust. In contrast, I'm a woman. An orphan. A ward of the state, until relatively recently. And a woman of color. I already know we aren't believed as much as a man like Causey.

I climb a few steps, wobbling in my low heels, and take a seat. The chair is like the kind you'd find in a doctor's office, vaguely uncomfortable despite the thin cushion. A microphone protrudes from the wooden bench like a long, spindly finger—accusatory.

The judge's seat is clearly the highest point in the room, but he seems even higher now that I'm right next to him. He looks down at me through two half-curved spectacles. "What's your name?" he asks, brusque though not unkind.

"Jane Mendoza."

"Ms. Mendoza, do you solemnly swear that you will tell the truth, the whole truth, and nothing but the truth, so help you God?"

I swallow around the knot in my throat. I never imagined that I was someone who might lie or do anything to prevent justice, but I also never understood how it would feel to be threatened. It's not just me that Causey might injure in retaliation. It's Beau. And Emily. And Paige. I risk everyone by speaking the truth. "I do."

He nods to Lauren, who gives me a gentle smile. "Jane. Can I call you Jane?"

I manage a short nod, which probably doesn't

help. I'm supposed to appear likable and trustworthy, the way Joe appears. But that's the problem with people like him. He's a chameleon. He can change his appearance like it's a jacket. I can only be myself. And the real me, deep inside, is off balance and shaky right now.

"Jane. Can you describe the first time you met former Detective Joe Causey?"

"It was after the fire." The insistent beeping from the machinery comes back to me. "I was in the hospital. Smoke inhalation. Beau had stepped away, and I was resting. Causey came in and started asking questions."

"What kinds of questions?"

"Not about the fire. I thought he would want to know if we'd left the stove on or if we'd seen anyone hanging around the house. But he also seemed suspicious. He told me that a girl like me would…" My voice trails off. I don't know if I'm allowed to say this word in court. And I don't really want to say it, either. "He told me that a girl like me would be with Beau Rochester for money."

"What did he mean, *a girl like you?*"

"He didn't explain. I assumed he meant someone poor. And powerless."

"Objection," says the defense attorney, briefly

rising. "Speculation."

"Sustained." The judge.

Lauren nods and moves on to her next question.

She'd already prepared me for this. That she would ask that question, that the defense attorney would object. We rehearsed all the questions that Lauren has. She walks me through the next times I saw Joe Causey, the times that he would badger me, accuse me, and the time I found the rat on the front porch of the inn.

That, at least, he's already confessed to doing.

All of it establishes a pattern of bad behavior on the part of the former detective.

It's not always about evidence, Lauren told me during our practice session. *Even with that DNA, it isn't a sure thing. It's really about how the jurors feel about him. If they feel like he's a dirty cop, they'll believe he could murder someone.*

Finally, Lauren gives me a smile filled with sympathy. "Thank you, Jane. No further questions."

I believe she does her work because it's the right thing to do. But I also believe what Beau said about her. She's using me. I'm a pawn in her case, but I'm a willing pawn.

The defense attorney stands. He has black hair

slicked back. His tie is a shiny purple paisley. His features are handsome in a magazine model kind of way. Everything about him feels slimy to me, but I have the sense that he's very successful.

That for some reason, only I'm seeing the slime.

"Ms. Mendoza," he says, a note of condescension in his voice. "The house fire you mentioned. Where were you when the fire started?"

Lauren is on her feet in black leather stilettos before he finishes his sentence. "Objection. How is this relevant?"

The defense attorney gives the judge a smile as if they have an inside joke. "I'm getting there."

"Quickly, Mr. Campbell."

"I'll ask again," he says, facing me. "Where were you when the fire started?"

"In my room. Sleeping."

"Alone?"

"Objection," Lauren says again, louder this time.

"I'll allow it," the judge says, but he gives Campbell a warning glance. "For now."

"No," I say, my voice breaking. I clear my throat. "I wasn't alone."

"Who was with you? Paige, the child you were in charge of caring for?"

"No." I want to stop there, but I already know he won't let me. I knew this would come out. This is the price I pay for telling the truth. But even if he didn't ask a follow-up question, I spoke an oath. I swore to tell the whole truth. "Beau was with me."

"Beau Rochester," he says. "Your boss."

"Yes."

"A man fifteen years older than you."

"Objection," Lauren says.

"Sustained," the judge says to Campbell. "Move on."

"This was relevant to Detective Causey's investigation of the fire. After all, both of you had an alibi. Each other."

"We didn't set the fire." Lauren had warned me the defense would play dirty. And it's happening. I've been afraid all morning. For days, really. Ever since I called Lauren and told her I'd testify. Though I find now that being faced with the questions, I don't feel fear. I feel anger. Anger that it's so hard for victims to get justice. That they have to be tormented by slimy defense lawyers to speak.

"Maybe you didn't set the fire," Campbell says, though he sounds doubtful. "But you can't speak for Beau Rochester."

"He was with me."

"The entire night? If you were sleeping, how do you know he didn't slip away?"

"What does this have to do with your client murdering Rhys Rochester?"

He smiles as if amused by my attempt at a rebuttal. "I'm the one asking the questions, Ms. Mendoza. You claim that Joe Causey said a girl like you might be with a man like Beau Rochester to get his money."

"He did say that."

"And did you?"

"Did I what?"

He turns to face the jury. "Did you get Beau Rochester's money?"

Heat spills over my cheeks. "You could say that."

"Spell it out for the court, please." He looks at the judge, warding off any potential objections. "If the victim's brother paid her off, then that brings the validity of her testimony into question."

Shame rushes through me. It's taught, this shame. The way society calls a man who sleeps around a player. But it calls a woman a slut. The way it gives a high five to a man who sleeps with a younger woman. But calls her a gold digger. I'm not ashamed of what I share with Beau, but I've been taught that sex is dirty. "Yes, I have some of Beau Rochester's money. He paid me very well for being a live-in nanny to his niece. He also pays for my college tuition. And he gifted me half the house we share together. Because we're in love. And you and Joe can try to make that sound as tawdry as you want, but the truth is, when you love someone, you don't care about money."

In the seconds that follow I remember my own declaration to Joe Causey. *Not everything we do is for money,* he said.

You're young, Ms. Mendoza, he responded. *Perhaps you still believe that.*

"That's quite a bit of money," Mr. Campbell says, with an expressive gesture toward the jury, as if to say, *see? I told you so.* "And this money is all out of... love, you say? Not for the sex. And not for your testimony today?"

"He doesn't even *want* me to testify. Why would he pay me for it?"

"This is a murder trial, Ms. Mendoza. If Detective Causey didn't kill Rhys Rochester, then maybe his brother did."

CHAPTER TWENTY-SEVEN

Beau Rochester

HERE'S A PART of me that's not civilized. No, it's quite savage. Like a caveman. And that part of me wishes I'd tied Jane up inside my cave so she could never testify. Free will be damned. Look at what's come out of it?

Jane's been in a state of anxiety ever since the courthouse.

It makes me want to strangle Joe Causey. That part is probably a normal human reaction. The world would be a better place without him. The abnormal part of my reaction is the intense need I have to… lock Jane down. To put her away somewhere safe. To keep her away from the world.

I know it's wrong.

People have free will. They can make their own choices. And the choice Jane made, to testify even though it put her at risk, even though it exposed her private life, was an admirable one.

But I can't shake the urge to bind her to me in some permanent way.

In the darkest shadows of my mind, that looks like actual bondage to a bed. I don't just feel that way because she's a woman. I feel that way because she's mine, and I have this primal need to protect her.

In a more practical sense, it's marriage. I would propose to her right now if I thought she'd accept. She loves me, but she's made it clear that she would like more time—more time as a college student, figuring herself out, before we get engaged.

Hell, even a wedding ring wouldn't be enough for me.

I want her pregnant and barefoot in the kitch-en. Like I said—caveman.

Of course, I know better than to tell her this. She'd run away from me, and no one could blame her. I don't tell anyone, not even Mateo.

It's a dark secret I harbor, that I'm really no better than my brother.

She's in her office, hiding behind a stack of textbooks.

Classes don't start for several months. That

doesn't stop her. After testifying, she's thrown herself into studying. She doesn't even have a class schedule yet, but she found the syllabi online that the professors used in previous years. They list the textbooks and the journals and the supplementary reading material. She's probably going to have them memorized forward and backward before she starts. She's scribbling notes in the margin right now, beside old notes already there.

These are secondhand textbooks with notes and highlights on the pages, with frayed binding. I couldn't talk her out of it. She refused to buy new books. That fucking defense attorney got under her skin about the money.

"Dinnertime," I say, leaning against the doorframe.

I don't really expect her to get up, and she doesn't. She briefly lifts her eyes, which are red from lack of sleep. "I'm still working. Don't wait up for me. I can just grab a snack before I go to bed."

Five days. That's how long it's been since the courtroom. And for five days, I've tried to coax her to eat and sleep. For five days I've tamped down the overprotective urge to lock her in the basement.

That ends now.

"You're done working for tonight."

It takes a second for the words to register. She lifts her head. "Why?"

"Because you're exhausted. Because you're punishing yourself for the bullshit that the defense attorney said to you. Because I want to hold you down and fuck you. Any number of reasons. Take your pick."

A slow blink. "If I'm so exhausted, then why are we going to—"

She has the same stricken expression on her face, the way she looked on the witness stand when she started to repeat what Joe Causey said to her. He made her feel ashamed of what we do together, and for that alone, I could kill him. "To fuck? Trust me, sweetheart. You aren't going to have to lift a finger. I'm going to do all the work."

"I'm not punishing myself," she says, pushing the book aside. "It's for school."

"Which doesn't start until the fall. I'm pretty sure you're supposed to read the books during class, not before it starts."

"I don't care about what Campbell said to me."

"Little liar," I say, pushing away from the doorframe and prowling across the room. "He got into your head."

She looks away. "I hate to think I could have ruined the case."

"You didn't ruin the case. The case is fucked up because Causey is a dirty cop with lots of money and friends in high places. You did what you could, but you don't control the criminal justice system."

"But why?" she demands in a sharp burst, so unlike her recent lassitude. "Why are they allowed to make people feel small and afraid? Why does the justice system help them do that?"

My stomach clenches. God, to have my hands on Causey for five minutes. At this point, I'd take his lawyer as a cheap substitute. "Because rich white men made the system. And they made it to help themselves."

Tears are in her eyes. "You're a rich white man."

"Yes. I am. And I'm sorry. I'm sorry the system is fucking broken. I'm sorry they got to do that to you. I'm sorry—hell. Do you remember that time in my office? When I made you suck my cock? When I made you come rubbing your sweet little cunt against my shoe?"

Her cheeks are a deep red now, and her eyes, they burn with desire instead of exhaustion. "How could I forget?"

"I'm going to return the favor." I drop to one knee as I say it.

I'm kneeling in front of her.

It's a five-thousand-dollar ergonomic chair because I knew, I knew even before the court-room, that she would be the most dedicated student. She'll spend countless hours on this chair, but from this night forward, it will always be tinged with the knowledge that I made her climax here.

Her eyes widen. There's nervousness. She's never felt completely comfortable with me licking her cunt. There's curiosity, too. She's wearing a T-shirt and jeans—comfortable clothes. Not seductive clothes, but she's still never looked hotter to me.

I push her knees apart and press my body between them. It makes her spread them wider, the breadth of my hips. We're close this way, my chest to hers, my mouth to hers.

A soft kiss, almost chaste. That's how this begins.

It loosens some of the tension in her shoulders. There are still knots in her muscles. They're going to be completely gone by the time I'm done with her. I start moving over her clothes, mouthing over her nipple through the thin fabric.

She's not wearing a bra, and my cock jumps at the feel of her nipple hard against my tongue.

Lower, lower. To the smooth skin of her stomach. I lift the hem of her T-shirt and suckle at her sensitive skin. She squirms against the chair, and it makes a breathy ergonomic sound.

She starts to reach for me, to move, to help, but I force her hands to the curved arms of the chair. "Hold still," I tell her. "You're not lifting a finger, remember? I'm doing all the work."

Her hands grasp the chair hard enough that her knuckles turn white. "Please."

I undo her jeans and tap two fingers against her hips. "Lift."

She's not wearing anything beneath the denim. No panties. The sight of her bare cunt makes my cock hard as a rock. Predictably, it wants to be inside her. Her mouth. Her pussy. Anywhere warm and tight. I force myself to go slow, pulling the denim down until it's free from her. She's naked from the waist down. She's still wearing her thin T-shirt, but it somehow looks even more illicit this way. Her nipples are hard knots beneath the fabric.

She's still tense. Still nervous. This is new to her.

God, everything has been new to her. I'm an

animal for fucking her when she's been anxious and emotional, but this is how I can connect with her. This is the only way I can show her what's happening inside me. I stroke my fingertips over the outside of her thighs and down her calves. And then move upward, inward, seeking that warm treasure.

She gasps when my fingers brush her folds. I have to tamp down a groan.

I tug her ass down to the edge of the chair. It's the only way her legs can get wide enough to loop over my shoulders. And then I lean in and fast myself on her.

Her clit. That's where I start because I'm not playing right now. I want her to feel this. To feel me. To shake with pleasure. Only then, when she's close, do I stop and work my way down. Already liquid has started to escape. I lick it up, hungry, desperate for this, savoring the musk of this woman, groaning with satisfaction when I'm met with more wetness.

"Do you know how much I want you?" I say between strokes of my tongue.

She cries out, unable to speak.

With every stroke of my tongue, I show her the power she has over me. It may be too little, compared to the injustice society has forced on her. It may be too late after I made her get on her knees for me. But it's honest. As honest as she was on the witness stand. She has power over me. Even though I want to lock her away, I'm the one in chains. I belong to her.

"Do you know how much I need you?" I demand, pushing two fingers inside her cunt, feeling her muscles contract around me. She's close. I've been holding her back from climax, but soon she'll go over. "Too much. Enough that it makes me into a terrible person."

"No," she gasps out.

I lick her again, harder with the flat of my tongue in retaliation. "Yes. I want to lock you up so that Joe Causey and his asshole lawyer can never even look at you, much less talk to you."

She moans because I've found that spot inside her that makes her writhe. I open my jeans and let out my cock, stroking it roughly, punishing it the way she punished herself with her books.

"Do you want to know about the man you let into your life?" I'm sharing too much, but I feel intimate licking her pussy, I feel spread open when I'm on my knees. "I want to put a baby inside you. You aren't ready yet. I know that, and I respect you, but I want it anyway. Because then you'd be mine. You'd never leave. The same way Emily would never leave Rhys."

Her eyes widen. "What? No."

I flick my tongue against her clit, and she bucks her hips against my face. "Yes," I say, my voice gravelly. God, it feels like heaven. And hell, having my secrets exposed to her.

She lets go of the chair and grabs my hair instead. Her hand tightens into a fist. The power she wields over me, it's real. As real as anything. She could stop this, stop the sex we're having, the game we're playing. Instead she raises the stakes. She pushes my face against her sex and presses her hips up at the same time. I spear my tongue inside her, and she gasps, but she doesn't lose focus. "You are *nothing* like him, Beau Rochester."

I grunt. That's enough of a disagreement, but I don't stop pleasuring her.

Her cheeks are flushed. Her eyes are glazing over with pleasure, but she keeps fighting. "You're a good man. And you're mine. And I'm yours. I'm never leaving you, Beau. Never."

On the final word, it turns into a high keening sound.

She comes against my mouth with a flex of secret muscles and a rush of wetness. I groan as my own orgasm takes over my body.

I can only fist my cock as it crashes through me, as my seed spills onto the wood floor in front of her chair like a carnal offering to a goddess.

CHAPTER TWENTY-EIGHT

Emily Rochester

THE ONLY THING it's possible to focus on is Joe's trial.

I can't think about what happened with Mateo. Or—I've thought about it so many times that the argument I'm having with myself has worn thin.

I want him.

I can't want him.

I need him to come back.

I can't ever ask him for that.

I should go to his house.

I can't go to his house.

I'm frustrated every time it comes to mind, which is constantly. I haven't had a moment of peace since I asked him to leave. He said he loved me, and I asked him to leave.

Even if I drove to his house, what would I say?

I know what happens when people fall in love. It's bullshit. All kinds of things happen. My life story isn't the only one. Plenty of people fall in love and don't get abused by their husbands. Plenty of people don't leave one brother for the worse one.

"Can I go to the zip line?" Paige asks. She's been drawing in the living room. A brand-new pack of colored pencils, delivered by Beau earlier this morning. "Mom? Can I? Can we both go?"

"Of course we can." I pick up my phone from its spot on the kitchen counter and open the local news app. It's not fancy, but I can keep a live feed on my screen while Paige and I go outside. Nobody's expecting a verdict this early, but I'm not going to be caught by surprise.

We go out across the lawn and Paige hops on her zip line. "I'm ready!" she shouts.

I swing her toward the other side and she flies away. My heart drops every time this happens. I know she'll be all right. She's had plenty of practice. But watching my daughter soar away from me hits too close to home.

Jane: *How are you holding up?*

The text makes me feel slightly less alone. Slightly less like a screwup.

Jane's sweet, though. She'd probably still send

this to a person who was an utter failure. Me? I just don't know what the hell to do with my emotions. I don't know why Mateo saying that he loved me sent me back to this place.

I do know why. Because it went so badly before.

But it hasn't gone badly with Mateo. It's gone better and better as the days pass. I've never had so much fun in my life as I did when we were in Disneyland Paris.

Jane's not talking about Mateo. At least, I assume she's not. I don't know what Mateo did after he went home. He could've shown up at Beau and Jane's house the next day and told them everything.

> **Emily:** *I just wish it was over. I'm ready to move on.*
>
> **Jane:** *I get it. I hope there's news today. See you guys tomorrow? Headed out in a minute for the meetup.*
>
> **Emily:** *Paige wants a rematch!*
>
> **Jane:** *Tell her she's on. ;)*

Paige always wants another game of Monopoly with Jane or Beau or even Mateo. She wants a game of Monopoly with everyone.

I try my best to live in the moment. I take

pictures of Paige on the zip line. Jane sends a few more texts. It's a very tentative, polite conversation, but it's good. If we're going to be next-door neighbors for any length of time after this, we have to be able to chat.

My heart aches and aches.

He went too far, too fast. That's the truth of the matter. Mateo Garza isn't in love with me. A trip to Paris isn't falling in love. Sleeping together isn't falling in love. Knowing a person down to their core—that's love. And Mateo has no idea who I am.

Bullshit, says the voice in the back of my mind. He might be the only one who knows you.

He's the one who sat on the couch with me during Joe's interview. He's the one who saw me. He's seen the sacrifices I've made and the things I've dealt with. He's seen everything. Mateo has been there when no one else was.

When Paige was missing in Disneyland, he knew what I needed.

So what if he doesn't know all the thousand incidental things that I haven't had time to tell him? Maybe he doesn't know what my favorite color is or what my all-time favorite restaurant is. What does that matter in comparison to the rest?

"Look, Mom. Mom. Mom!" Paige swings by

again, one hand waving in the air. I wave back at her. Snap pictures. Worry.

What if it's not him? What if Mateo isn't the one who has this all wrong? What if I'm the one who has a distorted view of our situation?

What if I can't love him the way that he loves me?

Like it or not, part of me is always going to be affected by my experiences with Rhys. I might always back away when I feel threatened. He would have to understand that. He would have to understand that it's not him personally. It's not his love that scared the shit out of me.

It's my own.

The realization brings me up short. Paige shouts for me again, but I hardly see her as she speeds past me.

It's not Mateo who scares me. It's not even his confession of love.

It's me.

All this writing and all this thinking I've done, and I didn't see it. I didn't see what I was hiding from.

I don't trust myself. I don't trust these feelings I'm having for Mateo because I don't believe, deep down, that I know what the hell I'm doing when it comes to men. Beau wasn't right for me, as much as I loved him. Rhys was dangerously wrong.

Mateo feels right.

He feels so right that I went to Paris with him. I got excited when he arrived at Paige's birthday party. Every time he kisses me, it feels like someone's turned a light on where I thought there could be only darkness.

"I'm not going to fall, Mom," Paige shouts as she goes by. "I know how to do this."

"Of course you do. You've always been brave."

The words come out of my mouth as automatically as anything I've said to Paige. They're ingrained down to my bones. She's always been brave. She's always been brave, and stubborn, and amazing. Of course she knows how to do this.

Why the hell do I think that I don't know how to do this?

I drop my phone into the grass and stretch my arms above my head. A weight has been lifted. A ridiculous mental weight that I made up for myself. I've been clinging to it for so long, and it's not even true.

My God, it's not even true.

If I didn't know how to do this—how to trust myself—I wouldn't have Paige back. I wouldn't have gone to Houston to convince Jane to help me. I wouldn't have met with Beau when we got back.

I know how to do this.

I shove aside all my fear and all my guilt and all the shit from the past that's been weighing me down. I pretend, for once in my life, that I'm on a zip line with Paige. Soaring back and forth. Confident in myself.

What do I feel about Mateo?

I feel… astonished. That's how I feel. Astonished that I never noticed him before. How could I not have noticed him? Because I was drawn to Beau's brokenness. The way he didn't want to give himself up to anyone else. Beau and I were too similar, I see now.

And I never thought I deserved someone like Mateo. Why would I? I was a woman who did wrong. I didn't wait for Beau when he went to LA. I let Rhys talk me into being together. When he turned out to be a monster, it seemed almost fitting.

Of course that's not true. I didn't deserve what he did to me. I deserve to be happy.

"Mom. Mom!" Paige plants her feet in front of me. "Are you sad?"

"No. Yes." I am sad. I'm happy. I'm relieved.

I don't have to hide from this. Why did I think I had to hide from this? "I'm having a bunch of feelings right now."

I reach for my phone and pluck it from where it landed in the grass. Mateo. I'll call Mateo. Or one of my friends. I need to get this revelation off my chest. I need to describe it to another person. A friend is probably best.

The news app is still open on the screen.

SURPRISE IN EBEN CAPE MURDER CASE

My stomach turns. I scramble for the buttons on the side of the phone. I feel like I've never used it before. Never used any phone before. I need to get the volume turned up so I can hear what the news anchor is saying. I need to hear that he's guilty.

He is guilty. I watched him kill Rhys. I was there.

"Mistrial," says the news anchor. She says more, but that's the only word I hear. It bangs around in my head. Mistrial. Mistrial. That's not the same thing as a not-guilty verdict. It means something went wrong. A technicality, usually, but he can be tried again.

But it does mean... "Former Detective Joe Causey was released from the county prison immediately following the determination by the court."

The rest of her sentence fades into cold, sharp fear. It's summer, but I'm frozen to the core. Shattered. The yard seems massive and undefended around us. I turn in a circle, looking in every direction for the bodyguards. I see one of them in the distance. It's not enough.

It's not ever going to be enough.

They're releasing him.

How?

He's guilty.

I could scream.

I don't.

Paige is here, and I don't want to upset her. It's inevitable, though, isn't it? I'll have to tell her that her murderous uncle is free in the world. I'll have to make a plan to get us out of here. I'll have to abandon our new house and find a way to live without him tracking us down.

A harsh laugh tears out of me. It's the same situation all over again. Only my brother might be worse than Rhys. He'll want revenge, and he won't stop until he has it.

He watched me testify.

He watched Jane testify, just the other day.

Neither of us is going to be safe.

"Mom?" The trembling fear in Paige's voice brings me back down to earth. "What are you doing?"

The fear in Paige's eyes doesn't banish my own, but it makes it manageable. I have no choice but to manage it for my daughter.

We're together now.

I go to her and brush her curls back from her forehead. "It's a little hot out. Do you want to go inside and have lemonade?"

She cracks a smile. "Can we also have muffins?"

"Yes, we can." Muffins and blue skies forever. I take her hand in mine and she lets go of the zip line. I hope she doesn't see the tiny earthquakes of fear moving down my spine. I hope they never enter into her memory. I hope this day remains perfect in her thoughts. "Do you want to see how fast we can run?"

I hate having to turn this into a game, but there's no better alternative. Every instinct I have is screaming at me to get us inside the house. To lock the doors and stay away from the windows until I can make a plan. Stay inside, stay quiet. There has to be a place on earth where I won't have to do this. I have to find it. I will find it. But the first step is getting back to the house.

Paige's eyes go wide, the blue there sparkling with excitement. "Where are we running?"

"Home," I tell her. "Our house. Kitchen door. Ready?"

"I'm ready," Paige shouts. "One, two, three. Go!"

CHAPTER TWENTY-NINE

Mateo Garza

I DON'T WANT to answer Catrina's calls. It's the last thing I want to do. But when she calls a third time, I can't put it off any longer. I pace to the other side of the beach house's porch and answer.

"Hi, Catrina."

"Mateo." It's quiet in the background. She's in her office, then, or holed up at her house. I don't care. I'm at the beach house I rented. I'm not with Emily. This seems like the most fundamental problem in my life. I'm not where Emily is, and I hate it. I'd rather not be in this situation at all. "I know you don't want to have this discussion, but we have to have it."

"The same discussion we've been having for weeks."

"Yes." Catrina's exasperated. As if I haven't

told her every goddamn time we talked that I wasn't going to do this. "The deal is now or never. I just need you to understand that word has gotten out. These things are never a secret for very long, and everybody in town is watching to see what you'll do."

By everybody in town, she means everybody in LA. I don't know how to explain it any more clearly. Everybody in LA doesn't matter at all to me. If they don't like my business decisions, they can find another up-and-coming actor to take my place. That's the way of things. There are always new people striving to make a life.

Emily's the only one who matters to me, and I think I've broken things between us. Maybe forever. Every second on this phone call with Catrina feels like a waste. If it's not solving things with Emily, then I can't force myself to care.

"This is a do-or-die opportunity." Catrina puts on her serious business voice. "And I mean that literally. Take this deal and it'll make your career. Turn it down and—"

"And it'll break my career?"

She doesn't laugh. "Yes."

Maybe she's right. Maybe she's not. I don't think it's as cut and dry as she's making it out to be, but I can't be bothered to care. "Okay, then.

I'm out."

"You're... out?"

"Yeah. I'm out. I'm done."

I just don't care. I can't bring myself to care about this deal, or that movie, or producer credits. What the hell kind of life is that? Endless publicity lunches and tours around the world with people I don't care about?

"Then I'm done representing you." A series of rapid-fire clicks. Catrina's typing. No doubt it's a message to her assistant to have her send me a termination letter. "You're finished in Hollywood, Mateo. I hope you've thought this through, because—"

A notification pops up on my phone.

EBEN CAPE COP MISTRIAL

What the fuck?

I hang up on Catrina mid-sentence. No more time for that. She's not my agent anymore. Maybe I'll never have an agent again. Fine. I stab my thumb on the notification until the full article opens.

They're going to let him walk free. Some bullshit about a technicality. I don't take the time to understand the full legal ramifications. All I need to know is that he's going to be on the streets of Eben Cape.

I don't give a damn if Emily's mad at me. I sprint through the beach house, fling the front door open, and run to my car. I don't bother going back to lock up. Take all the stuff inside. I'll replace it. All of that shit can be replaced.

Emily can't.

I break every speed limit on the way to the cliff. Liam North is waiting at the checkpoint at the bottom of the road. "I have to get up there," I shout out the window. "I have to see her."

"Emily's fine," Liam says. "We've got this place locked down. I heard the news."

"She's fine?"

"Yes. But you can go on—"

I never hear him say *through*. I'm too busy gunning it up the road. Liam North can say she's fine all he wants. I want to see it with my own eyes.

To hell with what happened the other night. I don't care. I took things too fast, and I scared her. That was on me. What was I thinking, walking out of there without trying to fix it? I'm never going to make that mistake again. Never in my goddamn life.

I speed past Beau and Jane's house. They're not there. A college thing for Jane. I don't like that, either. They should be here, with the security.

It has to wait. I can't text Beau and drive at top speed to get to Emily.

When I pull up to her house, I know she's heard. No doubt in my mind. Because three of my security guards are waiting on the porch.

The one in the middle nods to me as I climb out of the car. "Is Emily inside?"

"She and Paige are inside, Mr. Garza."

I stride onto the porch and let one of the guards open the door for me. I'm not standing outside and begging to be let in. Not sending her a bunch of texts. I just go in. She can kick me out later if she wants.

"Emily?"

"We're in the kitchen," she calls back. I can hear the slightest shake in her voice.

I go into the kitchen.

Paige and Emily sit at the kitchen island, muffins on plates in front of them. They have glasses of lemonade. Paige takes one look at me and breaks into a grin. "Hi, Uncle Mateo. Want a muffin?"

I mean to answer her. I really do. Except the word *yes* sticks in my throat. I can't do anything until I've done what I came here to do.

Which is to go around the kitchen island, take Emily by the hand, and pull her into my arms.

She practically falls into me, her arms going around my waist, her head going to my chest. All her fear is strung through her muscles.

"There are three guards on the porch," I murmur into her hair. "Nobody's getting in here."

"I know they're not. But maybe that's a problem. You know—" A deep breath that sounds very much like she's trying not to cry. "If you never let anybody in, you just start believing that it's better to be alone. You just start thinking that you're the one whose judgment isn't good enough. That maybe you don't deserve to be happy."

"Emily—"

"I kept trying to keep everybody out." She pulls back and looks into my eyes. "I tried to keep everybody out because I didn't trust myself to know what I wanted. That's crazy." Emily laughs. It sounds relieved and bewildered and tired. "It's just crazy. I know what I want."

My heart is about to make a run for it. She could say anything right now. I have no idea what direction she'll go. All I know is that I want it to be me. Goddamn it, I want it to be me. But if it's not, I won't push her. I'm not an asshole like Rhys.

"Tell me what that is. I'd like to know."

Tears fill her eyes. "I want you, Mateo. I'm sorry for all the years that I—" Emily shakes her head. "I can't go back and change anything now. But I know what I want. It's you. I love you."

"You don't have to say that just because I said it first. I shouldn't have gone that far. I knew better, and—"

"Mateo. I love you."

It overwhelms me. Many, many women have said things to me over the course of my life. Beautiful, successful women who wanted things from me. Things. Like money or houses or vacations. Emily Rochester doesn't want that.

"I'm scared to death," she whispers. "This mistrial or whatever they've done—it's terrifying. I don't know what he's going to do when he walks out of that courtroom. He might be out already."

"You're safe here. The security has it handled."

"What I'm trying to say is that I want you here. With me. I love you, and I want you here. My life feels better with you in it. I hate how it feels when you're gone."

It's starting to sink in, and it feels like champagne. A metric fuckton of champagne, shooting through my veins all at once. "You love me."

"I really do," Emily says, and she laughs. "I hope you still feel the same way."

"I was coming here to tell you that."

"You were coming here because you saw the news."

"Yeah. And I only care about the news because I love you." I want to look into her eyes for the rest of my life. I want to have Emily Rochester within reach forever. "I'm not bullshitting you. I care so much about you that it keeps me awake at night. Do you know what that does to a man?"

Emily flicks her eyes toward the ceiling. "Is it making you worse at auditions?"

"I'm not going on auditions anymore."

"What?"

"I just fired my agent. Or she fired me. It doesn't matter. I don't have an agent, and you can try to make me go back to LA. I'll let you try, Emily. But it's not going to work. I'm not going back there. I'm staying where you are, even if I have to live in that beach house and drive here every day."

"Mateo." She swallows hard. "You cannot give up your career for me."

"I can do anything I want. I've done so many

action movies that I could stop working today and be more than fine for a century. All I want is to stay here with you."

"You always wanted to leave Eben Cape."

"I always wanted to run away from the fact that you were with an asshole when you could have been with me. I got what I wanted out of LA. There's nothing left for me there."

I can't even fathom it. Going back to my soulless apartment. Sitting through lunches with people who truly only care about money. That's all fine and good while you're on the hunt for money yourself, but it didn't buy me the things I needed. And I need Emily Rochester.

I don't think anyone saw this coming. Well, maybe Beau did.

"But I might want to stay." Emily laughs again, and it's so absurd that we're having this conversation, it's so adorable. It's so perfect. "I might actually like Eben Cape. Most of it, anyway. You don't want to be one of those couples that comes back and puts down roots like they couldn't find anywhere better."

I would be one of those couples if it meant being with her. Emily's presence in my life transforms everything else. The shit I used to be cynical about is turning out to be wonderful. All the things I worked so hard to get have lost their shine.

"No, I wouldn't hate to put down roots with you. Are you listening? I love you. I don't care where we live. We could live here. We could live in Sleeping Beauty's castle in Paris. Anywhere."

"I love you," Emily whispers, her eyes lit up like she's never been able to say this before.

Paige groans. "Can you hear each other? You're both saying the same thing."

"Oh, hey, Paige," I say, and she smiles at me, tickled at my stupid joke. "Do you think I could hang out here for a while?"

"Why? Do you want to paint rocks with me?"

I want to paint rocks with her in a world that's not being menaced by Joe Causey. I want to put my arms around Emily in a place where we never have to worry about Joe or his actions again. There are many things I wish were different about this moment, but there's one I wouldn't change for anything.

"Yes. There's nothing else I'd rather do."

CHAPTER THIRTY

Jane Mendoza

THE GROUP AT the café isn't prospective students anymore. It's not people who might go to Mainland College—it's people who *are* going to Mainland college. We're starting in the fall.

One by one, we got our acceptance letters. We filled out the form on the website to commit. We have a plan for when the leaves drop off the trees. All the students will come back to campus. And we'll be part of that.

Grace turns around in her chair as I approach the table. We're meeting on a warm afternoon on the back patio, a place with uneven bricks and charmingly mismatched chairs. The sunny afternoon light shines on Grace's purple hair. It's in lovely curls by her shoulders.

"Jane!" Grace pats the chair next to her, a

broad grin on her face. "I saved you a seat, future social worker. How was the drive over?"

"It was fine." My heart feels warm, actually warm, at the seat she's saved for me. She was waiting for me to get here. Knew I'd come. Staked out a chair for me. If that's not a sign of belonging, I don't know what is. I've found friends here.

She takes a sip of her coffee, which she prefers to take black. "We're talking about where we're going to live. I'm still debating. Dorm or off-campus house?"

"Dorm," says Kevin. "The off-campus houses are a rip-off. They're total shit."

The guy who wanted to play intramural soccer—Pete—table shakes his head. "Can't have a good party in a dorm room. Besides, the houses are cheaper once you split the rent."

"Partying is not the priority." Kevin is the one shaking his head now. "You need to set up a tiered study system. I'm telling you. It's the only way we're going to get through this."

"Kevin. No." Grace bops his hand with hers. "No more study systems, for God's sake. This is about drinking microbrews."

"And talking about our hopes and dreams," Kevin answers with a smile.

At the end of the table, Megan—who's going

into English and really wants to have a meetup here to talk about the citywide book club book— puts her chin in her hand. "I don't know. I might go with the dorm. It's easier with my student loans. And I can't really afford much of an apartment." She sighs. "What about you, Jane?"

The group gets quiet.

It's one thing to talk about student loans and complain good-naturedly about the paperwork. It's another to be more explicit about things we can and can't afford.

And… it's different now that the news has broken.

National news that includes me and Beau. Our relationship. Our finances.

If I didn't feel so painfully awkward, I'd laugh. It never occurred to me that I'd feel this way about having too much money. Noah and I grew up knowing how to sidestep conversations about money. We had excuses ready to go if and when someone invited us to an event we couldn't afford. We had tricks, like just ordering water or going to restaurants that had free breadsticks.

Beau is rich beyond anything I could have imagined back then.

He's rich beyond anything most of the people at this table can imagine.

I won't have to worry about affording a house or a dorm room or an apartment. I'm pretty sure Beau could donate enough money to the college to have a building named after him.

I'm not going to say a word of that to Megan. I know some of where she's coming from. I know what it's like to be priced out of nice apartments. At the same time, I would have loved to stay in a dorm. A dorm with friends would have been paradise for me.

"Oh—Jane's thinking about that online program, aren't you?" Grace says, her voice carefully casually. She's smoothing this over for me. "She's got family in Eben Cape."

Megan perks up. "That's right. Eben Cape's gorgeous. That little downtown. The ocean." She gets a gleam in her eyes. "Are you saying we could have a meetup there? Maybe a spring break getaway? I'd love to go cliff diving at some point."

I wrinkle my nose. "Wouldn't you rather go to Florida? Or anywhere warm?"

"We could do a finals week retreat," Megan says. "If you have a living room floor we could crash on. Study all night. Party all day."

"Sure," I say. That does not sound like a good way to study for finals, but Megan's eyes sparkle. What do I know, anyway? Maybe people learn better when they have fun at the same time.

Maybe everything is better when you have a group of friends like this one.

"You have to come to our meetups," Grace says. "I don't care if you're doing the online thing. You're not going to abandon us."

"Yeah." Pete leans forward over his microbrew. "You're not getting out of playing soccer with us. Everybody has agreed to at least one match in the fall. Everybody but Kevin."

"I have goals," Kevin insists. "I won't have time. Not if I want to make the dean's list."

"Don't you want to be well-rounded?" Pete needles. "Nobody likes a doctor who doesn't have any hobbies. Come on. You can kick a ball around with us once a week."

This feels good. Cautiously good.

She has family in Eben Cape.

That's a good enough explanation for this group of people. I don't have to justify myself to them. It's okay that I'm not taking the traditional path of living in the dorm and being on campus. I'm not cutting myself off from the college experience. I have it, right here. I'm accepted. I belong. And I love the sound of having family in Eben Cape. I absolutely love it.

"I need coffee," Pete says. "I was up too late

last night. Anybody else?" He waves off the chorus of orders. "Never mind. Everybody's getting black coffee. You can add whatever you want to it."

"Wait. I'll give you money." Megan reaches for her purse.

"This one's on me." Pete leaves before she can push any bills into his hand.

It's so nice. I can't stop smiling. We can do this for each other. Get coffees for the table. Drop by with food. These tiny moments are what make a group of friends. Small acts of kindness for one another. I'm so happy to be part of it.

It's a dream come true. A dream I didn't know I had, honestly. College used to be a goalpost. It was about working and getting good grades and moving on. That's what I thought. But it's not about that at all. It's about what you have in the here and now.

"You could go off-campus, Kev," Grace says. "There are some good houses."

"The dorms are so much more convenient."

Grace groans. "Yeah, but you'll be surrounded with other pre-med students. It's like living in a bubble. You need a different perspective."

"Goals," says Kevin.

"Goals are not life," she says. "A house means more freedom."

"A dorm means less bills," Kevin counters.

"What if you meet in the middle?" I ask.

"What, like, we both live in tents in the quad?" Grace jokes.

A movement in the corner of my eye catches my attention. A dark shape moving on the other side of the patio fence. Someone passing by. I'm about to ignore it. About to sink back into the conversation when the back gate bursts open.

"What the hell?" Megan says.

I can't say anything.

It's Joe.

Joe in his suit and tie from the trial, his eyes wild. A gun in his hand.

Someone screams.

It's chaos.

Joe's on a mission. He stalks through the tables, shoving people aside, and grabs my arm. His fingers dig in. I try to hold the edge of the table. He can't drag me out if I have the table with me. My fingers are too slippery. It doesn't work. He hauls me away from my chair. Grace is out of hers, shouting at the top of her lungs.

"Let go of her. What the hell are you doing?"

Joe backs up, but my friends aren't backing down. He's taking me toward the gate. Kevin runs around the table next to Grace. They're fighting with each other now. She's trying to get to me, and he's trying to put himself in front of her. Trying to get to Joe at the same time.

Another foot toward the gate. I dig my heels in. If he gets me in a car with him, I'm dead.

"Don't interfere," he says, in his loud cop voice. "You're obstructing a police investigation."

"You're lying to us, man," says Kevin. "You can't do this."

"Ms. Mendoza is under arrest."

"No, I'm not."

"You're coming with me," he growls into my ear. "You want your friends to live? You make them stop. You make them stand down, Jane. If they come one step closer, you're responsible for their deaths."

My heart's beating so fast I'm afraid it will stop completely.

I can't fight him in here. I can't fight him on this patio. Other people will get hurt. He means what he's saying. He'll shoot Grace and Kevin. And even if everyone else from our group survives, it will never be over for them. It'll hang over their heads.

Not here.

"Guys." I use my calmest voice. "Stop. I'm telling you. Stop walking."

Grace's mouth drops open. "Jane."

"Stop walking. Let me go. Grace. You have to let me go."

They stop, but Kevin's got both hands wrapped around Grace's arm. He thinks this is wrong. It is wrong. Nothing about this situation is right. But if I can keep them alive, then that's what I'll do. That's what I have to do. Joe Causey's not going to kill anyone else.

I'll be the only one.

I let him take me backward through the gate. The parking lot out back is adjacent to a narrow street. Joe picks up the pace. His fingers dig into my arm so hard I cry out.

"Shut up," he snaps. "Shut your goddamn mouth."

I can see where he's parked. See his car. That's where I die.

That car is where I die.

I feel the same calm I felt in the fire. I knew I was going to die then, too. I just knew. And this time, there aren't going to be any second chances to be wrong.

This is it.

He's too strong. My body knows, even if my mind doesn't. Joe is too strong. If I try to slow him down too much, he'll retaliate by shooting my friends. Deep down, I know it will be a pointless struggle. He's out of his mind with the trial and bloodlust.

We reach the car.

Joe doesn't want to put his gun down to open the door, but he doesn't have any choice. Through my thundering heart and the strange calm of certain death, I realize he'll have to let go of the gun. He can't let go of me. If he does, I'll bolt. I'll make him chase me.

It's broad daylight. It's a sunny day. People would see. It would get complicated, and messy. Where would I run? Somewhere that wouldn't put other people in danger. But he's not going to let that happen. No, of course he's not.

He doesn't let go. He shoves the gun into the waistband of his pants and reaches for the door handle.

The door opens.

This isn't how I want to die.

My body jolts back from the open door, fighting anyway. I don't want Kevin and Grace to die for this. I don't want anyone at the café to be hurt. But I don't want to get in that car. I know better than to get in that car.

Joe's hands shove at me. It's a losing battle. He's going to get me into that back seat. My muscles resist him, but I won't be able to resist forever.

I think of Beau.

He's the one image in my mind as Joe pushes and shoves and curses. Beau. He'll be devastated. He'll be so sad, and feel so guilty. He'll blame himself for this.

I know how it will look. It will look like anger, but it will be pure grief. It will be the rest of his life. My one regret is that I can't stop that from happening.

My one regret is that I can't kiss him goodbye.

CHAPTER THIRTY-ONE

Beau Rochester

WAITING FOR THE outcome of the trial has me on edge. Dropping Jane off at her café hasn't improved the situation. I can't keep my phone in my pocket. Can't stop checking for updates. I get in line at a bank down the block from the café. My car's parked in the lot back there, and I should have stayed, too.

I came to get some cash for my wallet. An errand to run so Jane could have a few minutes with her friends. The line finally clears. The woman behind the counter smiles at me. "What can I do for you today?"

I push the card with my account number over to her and set my phone face-up, close to me. "I need five hundred." Could have gone to the ATM for this, but it would take less time. I'd be interrupting Jane. She deserves some aspect of normalcy in her life. A coffee with friends that isn't dominated by some rich, grumpy asshole at the table.

"Sure. Anything else?"

Three news alerts pop up on my screen at once.

EBEN CAPE COP MISTRIAL
JOE CAUSEY WALKS FREE

I don't read the third one. The first two have date stamps of ninety minutes ago, and two hours ago. Two hours ago.

"Fuck."

"Sir?"

"Forget it." I reach across the counter and take my card out of her hands. Shove my phone in my pocket. How did I miss this? Why did the alerts take so damn long to get to me?

Why did I ever leave Jane by herself?

The café's not far, but I can't force myself to walk. I'm at a dead sprint by the time I reach the front door.

It's not right in here. One of the girls behind the counter is sobbing. People are staring toward the back door. A couple pushes past me. They're hurrying to get out.

"Jane." Heads turn, but none of them is hers.

She said she'd be out back. At the patio.

I'm there in seconds.

She's not.

There's a group of college kids huddled around a table. Two of them fight near the back gate. "It's not enough," a girl with purple hair shouts. "They're not going to get here soon enough. Kevin. Kevin. The cops aren't going to be here in time. We have to go out there."

"He has a gun. He could shoot us." His hands are flying over his phone. "I'm going to call again. But I'm not letting you go out there."

"You can't stop me," she fires back.

"Where is she?"

The girl's eyes open wide, and she points through the gate of the fence. It's busted open.

Beyond her, at the opposite end of the parking lot, I can see them.

Joe.

Jane.

He's got his hands on her.

Everything tinges red. I storm across the parking lot without looking for cars. He's trying to get her into the back seat. Jane's resisting. Digging her heels in. She's maybe a foot from the open door, and Joe's swinging her body.

He puts his arm around her neck for leverage.

"No," I shout at him. "Get your goddamn hands off her."

Joe whirls around, bringing Jane with him. He puts his gun to her head, his arm tightening around her neck. I'm made of adrenaline and anger. Nobody's going to touch her like this. Nobody's going to hurt her.

"I don't think so," says Joe. "I don't fucking think so. I'm taking her with me. I'm finishing this."

"Let her go."

"No. Maybe I'd like to see what's got you so pussy-whipped." I'm fucking sure he would. Joe's a goddamn nightmare. No one wants that.

"You and I both know she has nothing to do with this."

"She has everything to do with this." Joe's eyes are bright. Too bright. He's lost his shit. "This little bitch put me in jail."

"I put you in jail."

"You tried."

"No, I did. I went to the prosecutor and told her all kinds of shit about you. I told her everything. I told her you're a killer."

"So what if I am?"

"She laughed. She thought you were such a goddamn coward."

This, of all things, gets to him. The thought of a woman laughing at him behind his back. Joe's face clouds over with fury.

Now, I think. Now, now, now.

Jane elbows him in the gut. Hard. Joe grunts and steps back, but he's still got a gun. He still has a gun, and he's close enough to Jane to shoot and kill.

What's the point of being alive if you're not going to stop a bullet for the woman you love? There's no point. I rush toward Joe like he doesn't have a gun.

He shoots.

I hear it.

I feel the bullet enter. It's an intense pressure, a lethal pressure, but I don't slow down. I don't react at all.

I don't care about the bullet. I'm going to kill this motherfucker.

Joe's eyes widen, then widen again. They're the size of dinner plates when I tackle him. He expected the bullet to stop me, and it didn't. Nothing will ever stop me from protecting Jane.

I take him down to the ground and pin him by the throat. The asshole can't even keep his gun in his hand. I rip it away from his fingers and toss it into the bushes. There. Now my hand's free to punch him.

One hit, square across the face. He can't get up with my hand on his neck like this. He can hardly breathe. This piece of shit. I hit him again. My shirt's getting hot. Wet. Another blow to the face. Joe's nose is bleeding. I want to break every bone in his body. I lose count of the punches. I lose track of the pain. All those years of suffering. All those nights that Paige cried herself to sleep or screamed until she lost her voice. Jane, with his arm around her neck. I'll hit him until my hand gives out. Until my life's over. Again and again and again.

"Beau." Two hands wrap around the fist I'm using to end Joe's life. "Beau. Please. Stop."

"No."

"He's out," Jane says. She's so close. Her eyes shine with tears. There's a mark on her neck from where he held her. "He's out. Beau. Look."

I look down at Joe.

Oh—that's what she meant.

He's out. Unconscious. His eyes are closed, and his face is battered. But he's still breathing. Shallow breaths.

"Don't kill him," Jane pleads, her voice low, urgent. "Don't do that to yourself."

She's worried for me. Jane's scared I'll have a

black mark on my soul from killing a killer. I don't know if that's true, but I know she's right. I know it'll stay with me. It'll stay with Emily.

Not long ago, I would have said it was a worthless argument. I would have said that there was no soul worth saving. That I was already past redemption. I would have punched him one more time, even though he's not fighting back.

I would have done that. My life felt like a wreck. I felt like a goddamn monster.

And then I met Jane.

I don't know if that's proof of anything. I don't necessarily think it's evidence that I'm a good person. There's no evidence on the planet that could convince me I'm deserving of Jane Mendoza.

But killing Joe Causey would hurt her. It would make things hard for me, and it would hurt her, and I won't do it. I'm done with all that. I'm done with the anger and the grief and the fear.

I'm done.

I don't have to be that way anymore. I don't know who I'll be when all this is over. But... it won't be over, will it? This is how things start. You defeat the villain and put him in the past, where he belongs.

I climb off of him and stagger to my feet. Fold

my arms around Jane. It hurts when she hugs me back. Right—the bullet.

"I got shot," I mention.

"I know." Jane's shaking. "I saw. I thought—" Her voice gives out. Must've thought this would kill me. She should know that nothing on earth is going to stop me from getting to her. "We should get you to the hospital."

She starts to pull away, but I stop her. "Those kids called the cops. They'll be here soon."

"I could drive—"

"Just stand here with me."

It feels too complicated to walk to my car. All the thousand things she'll have to do to get it ready to drive. Adjusting the seat. Finding the damn hospital. No. I want her here, in my arms.

"I'm sorry," Jane says against my chest. "I shouldn't have gone to that meetup."

"Fuck that. You should go to every meetup. Next time I won't go to the bank."

"Not if it ends like this."

Joe's flat on his back, on the ground. It's not going to end like this. Not ever again. He's done, too. They'll make sure of it this time. He tried to kidnap her. I'll testify until they have no choice but to put him away forever. Her friends will testify. It's so sunny out. Really, the perfect day to stand in a parking lot and wait for the ambulance.

"Did he get anybody else?" I ask. There were a lot of people in that café. Starting to get light-headed. Probably blood loss. It might be a good idea to sit down, but I have a bad feeling about that. Sitting down seems like giving up.

"No," Jane says. "My friends tried to stop him, but he said he'd shoot."

"They didn't give up on you. That girl. Purple hair?"

"Grace?"

"The purple hair. She wanted to come out here and throw punches. I had it covered."

"Beau." Jane's getting worried. "I think we should leave."

"No, shhh."

"Don't shush me. You're bleeding. You've lost a lot of blood. You don't get to decide what to do right now."

"I meant—listen."

There's a siren in the air. Two sirens, actually. Or one siren and one cop car. None of these bastards had better be Joe's friends.

A few seconds later, a parade of emergency vehicles speeds into view. I was wrong. There are two ambulances. Joe doesn't deserve an ambulance, but I guess it's better if they keep him alive for his jail sentence.

People gather at the edges of the parking lot. We're becoming a scene. Let them look. Paramedics jump out of the ambulance and split off. Cops swing themselves out of cop cars. There are so many lights. Pretty fucked up, how nice those lights are. People like Joe Causey shouldn't get to drive around in cars like that. I guess that's over for him now. He won't be arresting anybody else after this.

"Where's the weapon?" one of them barks. "We had reports of a shooter."

"It's in that bush." I gesture vaguely toward the bushes. "I want to press charges against that motherfucker. He shot me," I say, in case it's not obvious. I must be covered in blood.

"You'll have to do that in the hospital." A paramedic has gotten in close when I wasn't looking. Two more of them join her. It seems like overkill, but I'm not a doctor. I'm just a guy who got shot in a parking lot. "We need to get him into the ambulance. Gunshot wound at close range."

Another one of them puts a hand on Jane's arm. "Ma'am. Come this way. We need you out of the way."

I'm not sure I could stop them. It's getting

harder to stand up with every second. But I'll be damned if they take her away. I'll be damned if they pull her out of my arms.

"No." I'm not letting go of her. Not now, not ever. "She's staying with me."

CHAPTER THIRTY-TWO

Emily Rochester

"**W**HAT WAS HE thinking?" Mateo asks as he drives, pushing the speed limit on the way to the hospital. He drives fast but with impressive handling. "What the actual fuck was he thinking?"

"Probably that Jane was in danger. Beau doesn't think that much in those situations. He just acts. It's probably a good thing that he did. I can't imagine what would have happened if he wasn't there." The thought of it makes me want to throw up.

"Admirable," Mateo says. "Yes. Maybe. But now he's in the hospital, so he could have made better choices. One that didn't involve him getting mortally wounded."

"Is Uncle Beau going to be okay?" Paige asks from the back seat.

"Yes," Mateo and I say at the same time.

I turn around to look at her, forcing a small smile. "He's going to be just fine, sweetie. He might need some time to recover, but he'll be okay. We're all going to be okay."

"I feel okay right now," Paige says, very seriously.

My heart clenches. "I'm glad to hear it."

The Causey trial was already national news. I'm sure the results of his arrest, which is happening in the same hospital on a different floor, will also be in the news. But the reporters haven't had a chance to swarm the hospital yet. When we pull into the parking lot we just see some women in scrubs talking and an ambulance with the doors open.

"I think we can beat them," says Mateo. As long as a freak thunderstorm doesn't stop us, I think he'll be right. I've never seen him this focused. The news about Beau came in, and he sprang into action. It's like when he wanted to go to Paris.

Mateo Garza won't stand for a problem left unfixed.

It's like he's reading my mind. "The paparazzi?"

"Yeah." He's steering us toward the hospital

from the main road. He barely pauses at a stop sign and cruises through to the parking area. Mateo throws the car into *park,* like he's bringing one of us to the hospital, like we're the ones who are hurt. "Don't see any. Are we ready?"

Paige is already unbuckled and about to climb out of the car. She's faster than both of us. It gives me hope. If she can be this brave, so can I. "Ready!"

"Let's go."

I take her hand, and we start walking to the hospital entrance. I hope what I said is true. I hope we don't go in to discover that Beau is in serious trouble. I hope that Joe didn't do permanent damage. He's done enough of that in his life. No one else should suffer because of him.

"Emily," someone shouts from off to the left.

I know that voice. I loathe that voice. Anger rises. Frustration. I'm walking into a hospital. Can't this asshole see that? I try to walk faster, but Paige's legs are shorter and I refuse to drag her along. We'll go as fast as she can go. End of story.

"No comment," I say. "And stay the hell away from us."

"This isn't private property, Emily." He's jogging in from God knows where to pester me and take photos of us. I hate this guy. I can't stand him. "As a journalist, I'm going to report the news. What's your opinion on the Joe Causey mistrial? We need to hear from you. He's your brother. And you testified against him. You must be worried he'll come after you."

"Get away from her," Mateo says, stepping between us and him.

I can't believe the balls on this reporter. I kicked him off my property once. I'll do it again. Later, when we're not trying to visit someone important to us.

"Back off, Garza," says the guy. "I came here to get a quote from Emily Rochester." He's got his camera out. He wants more than a sound bite. He wants a bunch of photos of me reacting to him. Photos of my daughter. Photos of Mateo.

"I'd recommend backing the hell up," says Mateo.

"Has Joe spoken to you since he was released? Is a family reunion in the cards?"

All of my focus is on reaching the entrance doors. All of it. I don't have time for this man. He can print whatever he wants about me. I'll have the final say in my book. I'll have the final say in my goddamn life. No asshole with a DSLR is going to take that from me.

"Last chance," says Mateo, but it almost

sounds like wants the guy to keep going.

"What does your daughter think about the case? Paige might—"

Mateo punches him, the burst of violence both fluid and shocking.

It's the cleanest hit I've ever seen. Hard and true. It gets the photographer in the nose, and the man crumples. It seems impossible that he's never been punched before, but he goes down like a tree. I've only ever seen Mateo calm and cool and charming. Never so angry he's lost his temper. It makes me stop and stare at him with my mouth open.

Mateo leans down. "I said back up. Can you hear me now?"

The reporter tries to scramble backward and is stopped by a decorative pot that's bursting with flowers. "I'm going to press charges," he gasps.

"I'm the one who's going to press charges," I say, recovering from my shock. "I was going to let your trespassing on my property slide, but I don't think I will. In fact, Mateo? Can you drive me to the police station? I want to get this on the record."

"Just stop." The reporter gets to his feet, one hand clutching his nose. "Stop. I'm leaving. Fuck's sake. I'll stay out of your way. Crazy bastard."

"Great," says Mateo. "I'm glad we understand each other."

"Uncle Mateo," Paige whispers. "You're not supposed to hit people."

He makes his eyes wide. "What? Are you serious?"

"Yeah. You can get in big trouble for making people get a nosebleed."

"Oh, man." Mateo rubs the back of his neck. "You think I'll get in trouble?"

Paige giggles. "No. I think people like you too much to get you in trouble."

We've reached the hospital doors. Paige reaches for Mateo's hand.

This is it, isn't it? This is how it starts. A family walking into the hospital. It's not the most ideal situation. I don't want Beau to be hurt. I don't want Joe to have gotten free. But I'll make sure that Beau is okay. And Joe is already under custody again.

Everything isn't right in this moment, but it's getting there.

"We're going in together," Mateo tells Paige, and he meets my eyes over her head. "You and me. And your mom. We're going to see Uncle Beau, give him a hard time for getting himself shot. And then we're going back home. Together. Are you good with that?"

A family. He saw it before I did, but then I had learned not to trust men. I'd learned not to trust myself, but that's changing. I'm stronger now. "Together," I say, putting my hand in his.

✧   ✧   ✧

Thank you so much for reading the Rochester series! If you love Beau and Jane, I have great news for you. You can get a bonus scene if you sign up for my newsletter...

GO HERE: www.skyewarren.com/rochester

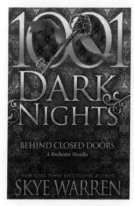 *You can also read the story of Marjorie, who owns the Lighthouse Inn...*

Marjorie Dunn is hiding in plain sight. The past can't find her at the peaceful inn she owns in a quiet coastal town in Maine.

Until Sam Brewer walks through the door. He arrives in the dead of night, with a dark suit and storm-gray eyes.

Marjorie knows better than to trust this stranger, but she can't resist his touch. Every kiss binds them together. Every night draws the danger close.

She risks her heart with him, but more than that, she risks her life.

The past has caught up with her. And it wants her dead.

Books by Skye Warren

Endgame Trilogy & more books in Tanglewood

The Pawn

The Knight

The Castle

The King

The Queen

Escort

Survival of the Richest

The Evolution of Man

Mating Theory

The Bishop

North Security Trilogy & more North brothers

Overture

Concerto

Sonata

Audition

Diamond in the Rough

Silver Lining

Gold Mine

Finale

Chicago Underground series

Rough

Hard

Fierce

Wild

Dirty

Secret

Sweet

Deep

Stripped series

Tough Love

Love the Way You Lie

Better When It Hurts

Even Better

Pretty When You Cry

Caught for Christmas

Hold You Against Me

To the Ends of the Earth

For a complete listing of Skye Warren books, visit

www.skyewarren.com/books

ABOUT THE AUTHOR

Skye Warren is the New York Times bestselling author of dangerous romance. Her books have sold over one million copies. She makes her home in Texas with her loving family, sweet dogs, and evil cat.

Sign up for Skye's newsletter:
www.skyewarren.com/newsletter

Like Skye Warren on Facebook:
facebook.com/skyewarren

Join Skye Warren's Dark Room reader group:
skyewarren.com/darkroom

Follow Skye Warren on Instagram:
instagram.com/skyewarrenbooks

Visit Skye's website for her current booklist:
www.skyewarren.com

COPYRIGHT

This is a work of fiction. Any resemblance to actual persons, living or dead, business establishments, events or locales is entirely coincidental. All rights reserved. Except for use in a review, the reproduction or use of this work in any part is forbidden without the express written permission of the author.